Winter will be over soon and we have new books guaranteed to put a spring in your step! Lose yourself in an absorbing read from Harlequin Presents....

Travel to sophisticated European locations and meet sexy foreign men. In *The Greek's Chosen Wife* by Lynne Graham, see what happens when gorgeous Greek Nikolas Angelis decides to make his convenient marriage real. *The Mancini Marriage Bargain* by Trish Morey is the conclusion of her exciting duet, THE ARRANGED BRIDES—we brought you the first book, *Stolen by the Sheikh,* last month.

Fly to more distant lands for Sandra Marton's UNCUT story, *The Desert Virgin.* Feel the heat as ruthless troubleshooter Cameron Knight rescues innocent ballerina Leanna DeMarco. If you haven't read an UNCUT story before, watch out—they're almost too hot to handle!

If you like strong men, you'll love our new miniseries RUTHLESS. This month in *The Billionaire Boss's Forbidden Mistress* by Miranda Lee, a boss expects his new receptionist to fall at his feet, and is surprised to find she's more of a challenge than he thought. Lucy Monroe's latest story, *Wedding Vow of Revenge,* promises scenes of searing passion and a gorgeous hero.

The Royal Marriage by Fiona Hood-Stewart is a classic tale of a young woman who has been promised in marriage to a royal prince. Only she's determined not to be ruled by him and her declaration of independence begins in the bedroom!

We hope you enjoy reading this month's selection. Look out for brand-new books next month!

We're delighted to announce that

A
Mediterranean
Marriage

is taking place in

Harlequin Presents®

—and you are invited!

Imagine blue skies, an azure sea,
a beautiful landscape and the hot sun.
What a perfect place to get married!
But although all ends well for these couples,
their route to happiness is filled with emotion
and passion. Follow a couple's journey in the
latest book from this inviting miniseries.

M

Lynne Graham

THE GREEK'S CHOSEN WIFE

A Mediterranean Marriage

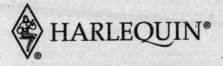

HARLEQUIN®

TORONTO • NEW YORK • LONDON
AMSTERDAM • PARIS • SYDNEY • HAMBURG
STOCKHOLM • ATHENS • TOKYO • MILAN • MADRID
PRAGUE • WARSAW • BUDAPEST • AUCKLAND

ISBN 0-373-12523-2

THE GREEK'S CHOSEN WIFE

First North American Publication 2006.

www.eHarlequin.com

Printed in U.S.A.

All about the author...
Lynne Graham

Born of Irish/Scottish parentage, **LYNNE GRAHAM** has lived in Northern Ireland all her life. She and her brother grew up in a seaside village. She now lives in a country house surrounded by a woodland garden, which is wonderfully private.

Lynne first met her husband when she was fourteen. They married after she completed her degree at Edinburgh University. Lynne wrote her first book at fifteen and it was rejected everywhere. She started writing again when she was at home with her first child. It took several attempts before she sold her first book and the delight of seeing that first book for sale in the local store has never been forgotten.

Lynne always wanted a large family and has five children. Her eldest, and her only natural child, is in her twenties and a university graduate. Her other children, who are every bit as dear to her heart, are adopted: two from Sri Lanka and two from Guatemala. In Lynne's home, there is a rich and diverse cultural mix, which adds a whole extra dimension of interest and discovery to family life.

The family has two pets. Thomas is a very large and affectionate black cat, and Daisy is an adorable but not very bright white West Highland terrier, who loves being chased by the cat. At night, dog and cat sleep together in front of the kitchen stove.

Lynne loves gardening, cooking, collecting everything from old toys to rock specimens and is crazy about every aspect of Christmas.

PROLOGUE

NIKOLOS ANGELIS STUDIED his father in rampant disbelief. 'You're not serious. You *can't* be serious. We own one of the biggest companies in Greece!'

Symeon, a handsome man with silvering dark hair, was not looking his ebullient best. His complexion was grey and heavy lines of exhaustion marked his features. 'I took a gamble and it didn't pay off. In fact, it was a disaster. The company is over-stretched and the bank is getting very nervous. They made me pledge everything we possess but they're still not happy. If they pull the plug now, we'll lose the lot!'

Nikolos said nothing. *Everything?* Even the family home? He was so angry that he did not trust himself to speak. His grandfather, Orestes, had taught him that a man should put the honour and security of his family first. While the old man had lived the family fortune had been in safe, protective hands. But Symeon Angelis didn't operate that way. Even though he was in his fifties, he was still desperate to prove that he could wheel and deal as successfully as his legendary father and he had lost millions pursuing high-risk deals.

'If it's any consolation,' Symeon muttered heavily, 'you were right about the Arnott development being too good to be true.'

Nikolos swung round, stung beyond bearing by that admission. 'You bought in even after the Kutras brothers warned you to stay clear?'

Symeon Angelis winced and gave his eldest son a rueful look. 'I thought they were trying to corner all the action for themselves.'

Nikolos ground his even white teeth together in silence. He did not allow himself to look in his parent's direction. He was ashamed of the fierce contempt he was feeling. Symeon was a good man, a good father, a good husband. He was universally well-liked and respected but his intellect was not powerful and he was a lousy entrepreneur. Nikolos, on the other hand, had devoted his spare time as a teenager to some highly profitable trading in stocks and shares that had made him a millionaire before he even left school. To stand by powerless and watch his less clever and shrewd father stumble and make stupid mistakes was, for Nikolos, a punishment of no mean order.

'I'll be frank with you. This may be our darkest hour but we have been offered an escape clause,' the older man confided in a taut undertone. 'It came from a surprising source. In fact, I was astonished… However, I said it couldn't be done. It wouldn't be right—'

Mastering his impatience, Nikolos rested grim eyes on Symeon. 'What wouldn't be right?'

His father seemed reluctant to meet his son's enquiring scrutiny. 'I can't ask you to make such a sacrifice at your age. You're only twenty-two—'

'What's that got to do with anything?'

Symeon Angelis expelled his breath in a hiss. 'Theo Demakis approached me and offered to bail us out.'

Nikolos vented a startled laugh of incredulity. 'Theo Demakis? Are you winding me up? Since when did we move in such exalted circles?'

'It seems that we could move in those circles if we wanted to,' Symeon murmured with the air of a man choosing his words with extreme care.

His son's lean, bronzed face stayed unimpressed. 'Demakis is as cold as a corpse. If you get into bed with him you'll wake up with a knife stuck between your ribs.'

'In other circumstances, that might have been my attitude as well. But Theo is offering a family connection rather than just a business transaction.'

At those words, Nikolos fell very still. 'You can't mean what I think you mean…'

The older man flushed a mottled pink. 'I can see where Demakis is coming from—'

'I think your view must be fogged—'

Refusing to be discouraged, Symeon pressed on. 'Theo's only son must be dead ten years now, he's on his third wife and he still doesn't have another child. He only has his English granddaughter. He wants Prudence to marry a Greek boy from a good background and that's not surprising when she's half-English and illegitimate into the bargain. Demakis is an old-fashioned man and he's offering an old-fashioned deal.'

An appalled inability to credit what he was hearing kept Nikolos silent.

'If you married her and there was a child, the world would be your oyster,' Symeon breathed tightly. 'Yes, it would save us, too, but you're ambitious and she'd be the equivalent of a golden goose. To talk of such an arrangement in terms of cold, hard cash is vulgar but it is only right that I should draw your attention to the very obvious benefits.'

Nikolos closed his eyes, lashes long and black as silk fans momentarily hitting his high cheekbones. He was disgusted by his father's willingness to consider such an arrangement. Prudence, whom his friends had christened Pudding for her love of baklava pastries, was to be his wife? He was shocked and outraged by the suggestion. He hardly knew her, although he had on several occasions intervened when he saw her being ignored and insulted at social events. Her lack of Greek and her trusting nature had made her a soft target, for no matter what was said to her she would assume it was pleasant and she would smile.

Her inability to defend herself had infuriated Nikolos. He hated bullies and would have done as much for any helpless creature too stupid to look after itself in a hostile world. But had those trivial displays of good manners, those minor acts of compassion on his part, led to the gruesome offer of Prudence's hand in marriage? That daunting suspicion made his lean, strong face clench hard. When he walked into a room, she lit up like a Christmas tree. Had Prudence decided to tell her fabulously wealthy grandfather just how much she fancied Nikolos Angelis?

'Papa…' Nikolos's sister Kosma's distraught voice cut through the simmering silence from the French window that opened out onto the terrace. 'I know I shouldn't have been listening and I'll die if we become poor but you can't ask Nik to marry Theo Demakis's granddaughter. She's a fat cow and plain as a pig!'

'How dare you hide behind the door and eavesdrop on a private conversation?' Embarrassment made Symeon Angelis leap up in a wrathful response that his much-indulged daughter had rarely witnessed. 'Leave us—'

'But it's true,' the pretty teenager wailed, standing her ground and defying his authority. 'Nikolos would have to put a paper bag over her head to eat at the same table, never mind anything more personal. She's ugly and he's so handsome—'

'Get out,' Nikolos told his kid sister with ferocious, cutting cool.

The older man watched his daughter retreat tearfully at her big brother's bidding and released a regretful sigh. 'Of course, I've never seen the girl. If she's that bad, Kosma would have a point. I couldn't ask you to marry her.'

Nikolos bit back a sardonic laugh. That this was the only objection his parent could see to such a revoltingly mercenary proposition spoke volumes for his father's state of mind. Symeon Angelis was fighting despair and ready to clutch at any straw that might drag him back from the abyss of financial ruin. Nikolos asked himself how he could stand back and allow that to happen to his parents and his four siblings.

Yet at twenty-two years old, he felt that his own life had barely begun. He was no innocent though, he conceded grudgingly. Even though he was still at university, he had acquired a reputation as a womaniser. It was true that he pursued pleasure with single-minded zeal. He worked hard and he played hard and he rarely slept alone. He didn't do long-term and he didn't do faithful. He had yet to meet a girl who would not accept those conditions. But he still could not begin to contemplate the prospect of becoming a husband or, worse still, a father. Indeed, the very concept of being forced into such a heavy commitment for his family's benefit filled him with seething anger and bitterness. But he also knew that his grandfather, Orestes, would have laid down his own life to protect his nearest and dearest...

'You remind me of my late son and his mother.' Theo Demakis studied his granddaughter with cold derision. 'You have the same puppy-dog eyes, the same scared smile. You've got no backbone and weakness disgusts me.'

'If I was weak, I would have gone home the day after I arrived.' Prudence tilted her chin, her soft blue eyes staying steady while beneath her loose cotton shirt she could feel her heart beating so fast with fear that she felt sick.

His unpleasantness continually appalled her. It was three weeks since she had come to stay on the older man's magnificent estate and every day had been an ordeal. Having flown out to Greece with naïve hopes of getting to know and love the grandfather she had never met, she had instead been forced to accept that he was a cold, malevolent man with not an atom of affection for her and a vicious tongue.

Theo Demakis laughed at her attempt to stand up to him. 'Do you take me for a fool? Why do you think I invited you to visit me? You've taken everything I've thrown at you because your mother's on the booze again and the bailiffs are back at the door!'

Dismay peeling away the composure she was struggling to maintain, Prudence could no longer hold his derisive gaze. As she dropped her head in shame-faced embarrassment, a curtain of chestnut-brown hair fell forward to screen her rounded profile and she looked very much her nineteen years.

'Am I right?' the older man sneered.

'Yes…' The admission almost choked Prudence, for she would have loved to tell him that he was wrong and that her mother, Trixie, had cleaned up her act and turned her life around. Sadly, that wasn't possible and her grandfather's contemptuous satisfaction made the humiliation of her mother's frailties sting even more. She suspected that he was congratulating himself on his foresight almost two decades earlier when he had told his son to ditch his pregnant girlfriend.

'What a winner Apollo picked to father my only grandchild with! He had the pick of the world's heiresses. He could have brought a royal princess home as his bride,' Theo Demakis growled in disgust. 'Even then I was rich as Midas and money is the equal of any fancy pedigree. But my son wasn't the sharpest knife in the drawer, was he? He picked a woman who was a lush, a spendthrift and a whore—'

Her face flaming, Prudence surged upright. 'I won't sit here listening to you talking about my mother like that!'

The older man surveyed her with ironic amusement. 'What choice do you have? You need my money to dig her out of trouble.'

At that blunt declaration, Prudence lost colour. She lowered her head and swallowed hard on her angry pain. Slowly, heavily, she sank back down in her seat again. As she had learned at an early age, penury and dignity rarely went hand in hand. In any case, Theo Demakis was right and the truth was not very pleasant: she *did* need his money. Her mother was deeply in debt, drinking heavily and currently facing court action over unpaid bills. But Prudence was convinced that if the stress of the older woman's financial problems was removed, Trixie could be persuaded to enter a clinic and go through rehab again. Painful as it was to accept, Prudence reflected with a sinking sensation in her tummy, Demakis money could well make the difference between her mother living or dying. Years of alcohol abuse had dangerously weakened Trixie's health.

The older man dealt his silent granddaughter a harsh look of impatience. 'I brought you to Greece only because I believe you can be of use to me. It'll be interesting to see if you have the brains to recognise a lucky break when it's on the table in front of you. '

Her brow indented, Prudence was bewildered by that statement.

'What do you think of Nikolos Angelis?' Theo asked with the teeth-baring smile that sent a shiver down most people's backs.

The disconcerting sound of that particular name shattered Prudence's composure. Blushing like mad in her confusion, she averted her attention from her grandfather without even noticing the chilling curl of his thin mouth. 'He's…he's kind,' she framed finally, biting back a whole host of other, more enthusiastic words which she felt would have exposed her to the older man's derision.

How could she possibly speak freely about Nikolos without revealing the depth of her feelings for him? She was in love for the first time in her life but that was her secret and she had no intention of sharing it with anyone. After all, Nikolos had the dark, dangerous beauty of a fallen angel and she was overweight and plain. It was a hopeless passion and she knew it.

'How do you think Nikolos will handle poverty? At this very moment, the Angelis family are facing financial ruin. They'll lose their homes, their cars, they'll have to take the younger children out of their fancy schools and that will just be the beginning of their sufferings. After more than a century of wealth and ease, his parents will find it very difficult to adapt to such heavy losses.' Theo watched the surprise and immediate concern blossoming in her expressive eyes. 'But you have it within your power to save them all from that unhappy fate.'

'How could I help them?' Prudence exclaimed, shaken by the picture he had drawn.

'By helping me. If you agree to marry the Angelis boy I'll rescue his family and also take care of all your mother's little problems. I will be very generous to all parties concerned and I am not a generous man as a rule.'

Prudence stared back at him in wide-eyed astonishment. As he spoke, her soft full mouth had parted several times as though she intended to break into speech but each time innate caution had made her hold back. 'Me…agree to marry Nikolos Angelis? How on earth could that come about? It sounds totally mad…and I don't understand how that would be helping you,' she framed shakily.

'There's method in my madness.' The portly older man poured a measure of brandy into a crystal glass. 'I want a male heir, but with the exception of your father my own efforts in that direction have been unsuccessful. However, you're young and healthy and so is the Angelis boy. If even half of the rumours about his virility are true, it shouldn't take him very long to achieve the required result.'

His coarse laugh made agonised colour well up below his granddaughter's skin. 'I can't believe you're talking to me like this,' she protested. 'For goodness' sake, Nikolos wouldn't marry me...he wouldn't want me—'

'It's not a matter of wanting, which is just as well, isn't it? You're no beauty,' her grandfather pointed out with a casual cruelty that turned her white. 'But, believe me, given the choice between marrying you and watching his precious family lose everything, Nikolos Angelis will take you as his bride—'

'No...' she muttered sickly, her hands tightly clenched in on themselves, for she was humiliated beyond bearing by his taunts.

'He will. He is not a fool like his father. He's strong and very loyal to his family. As for you, you do have Demakis blood in your veins and I'm giving you both a wonderful opportunity.'

'That's not how I see it...you're talking about blackmailing Nikolos into marrying me!'

The older man fixed his steely gaze on her. 'I dislike wild accusations. There is no blackmail,' he specified with cold clarity. 'I'm offering a helping hand in return for a favour. Turn your back on my generosity if you wish.'

'It's not a question of me doing that. Just please help me help my mother,' she begged him in desperation.

'Accept that I don't care whether your mother goes to

prison or drinks herself to death,' Theo Demakis fielded drily. 'Why would I care? What is she to me?'

'Trixie might not be in the mess she's in now if she hadn't had such a battle to survive when I was a kid!'

His scorn unconcealed, Theo Demakis checked his watch. 'Look out of the window…'

After a moment's hesitation, Prudence scrambled up and stared down at the pristine gardens. She wondered what she was supposed to see when her mind was in so much turmoil that she was incapable of concentration. Belatedly she noticed the taxi waiting by the imposing front door.

'That taxi is waiting to take you to the airport.'

Prudence was as startled by that announcement as he could have wished. '*Now*…you want me to leave?'

'Your luggage has already been packed. If you say no to marrying the Angelis boy, I will send you home to the UK immediately and you will never hear from me again. Make your mind up and do it quickly.'

A sense of panic gripped Prudence. 'Can't you be reasonable about this? It's so unfair to spring this on me and demand—'

The older man vented a cruel laugh of disagreement. 'I think it unfair that you should show no appreciation for the fabulous future I am prepared to buy for you. You have your choice. Run back to your mother and see how grateful she is when she learns that you could have made her financially secure for life!'

Prudence flinched at that crack, for she knew that Trixie would consider such a reward her due after the sacrifices her single parenthood had entailed. In fact she clearly saw what her grandfather was doing and recognised the pressure he was bringing to bear on her. She considered herself strong and resilient, but the certainty of his cold, unforgiving malice frightened her and plunged her into despair. She knew that he meant what he said. He really didn't care what happened to her and he would not give her the funds she needed to support her mother unless she did as he asked.

'This is crazy,' she muttered frantically. 'Nikolos would never agree to marry me in a million years! For goodness' sake, he's dating Cassia Morikis…'

Theo Demakis shrugged. 'So he's sleeping with the Morikis girl. What's that got to do with anything?'

Prudence blinked. 'I…I just thought that if he loves her—'

'So what if he does? That's nothing to do with you. He will decide his own options. He's Greek to the backbone. Believe me, family honour and practical, material considerations will be of much greater importance to him than the current slut in his bed.'

His cold-blooded indifference to her revelation and his careless reference to Nikolos's sex life shook Prudence to the core.

'Are you planning to take that cab ride to the airport?' Theo prompted with impatience.

Prudence went rigid, stress flaring through her small frame like petrol thrown on a fire. Nikolos Angelis would never agree to marry her, she thought feverishly. The very idea of them as a couple was ludicrous. Cassia Morikis was a very beautiful girl: tall and slender as a reed, she had glorious platinum-blonde hair and dainty, doll-like features. But why was she working herself up over something that was most unlikely to ever happen? Why was she daring to inflame her grandfather's temper with her objections? She had to keep her mother's needs centre stage in her mind; Trixie had first call on her loyalty and concern. Surely she could safely leave Nikolos to refuse the marriage proposition out of hand for both of them? Her grandfather could scarcely blame her for her prospective bridegroom's reluctance!

'Answer me,' Theo Demakis urged flatly.

'All right…yes, I'll stay.'

'I never doubted it. I was really quite touched by the romantic glow I saw in your face when I mentioned the boy's
name.' As a stricken look of pained embarrassment filled
Prudence's eyes, the older man laughed and tossed back his
drink. 'I feel like Eros, the god of love. My wealth will be your
dowry and at least it will save you from the humiliation of
being left on the shelf.'

That night, Prudence lay sleepless in her opulent guest-
room bed. The huge villa was silent. From the moment she
had arrived in Greece, to a world of luxury and privilege that
was as foreign to her as the hot climate, she had felt as though
she was living in someone else's dream. Not a pleasant dream,
either; more of a nightmare where everything—even the way
people behaved—was unfamiliar. She had done her utmost to
please her grandfather. That had meant stifling her natural
shyness and accepting the social invitations that he had organised in advance of her arrival. Eirene, the teenaged daughter of one of Theo's friends, had acted as her companion for
all of those painful outings into high society.

Prudence had stuck out like a sore thumb at those exclusive gatherings. Eirene belonged to an élite set of rich and
spoiled young people who dressed in the latest fashion, went
wild playing reckless games at parties and still contrived to
behave as though all the world was a bore. Prudence had
found them silly and superficial and the females had been horribly bitchy to her. Time and time again she had squirmed behind her fixed smile, never daring to retaliate, knowing she
could not risk offending anyone who might complain about
her to her grandfather. Not once had she allowed herself to
forget the central issue of her mother's desperate plight.

Trixie Hill had been a well-known catwalk model when she

met Apollo Demakis and fell in love with him. The young Greek playboy had showered her with expensive gifts and asked her to marry him. For over a year Prudence's fun-loving parents had jetted round the world from one party to the next. Trusting that her lover would soon be her husband, Trixie had put her career on hold. But when Trixie had fallen pregnant, Apollo Demakis had come under pressure from his father and had swiftly reneged on his promises. When Trixie refused to agree to an abortion, he had ditched her. But not before he reminded the mother of his unborn child that she had not been a virgin when they met and that she had acquired an unsavoury reputation from openly living with him before marriage.

In remembrance of those final insults which her unlucky mother had endured, Prudence's soft, full mouth curled with distaste in the darkness. The father she had never met had been a hypocrite, a liar and a creep. Trixie had had to go to court to prove her baby's paternity and after a lengthy battle had been granted a pitiful amount of child support which had frequently gone unpaid. Was it any wonder that her mother had started drinking too much? At the age of seven, Prudence had had to go into foster care for a while. A newspaper had run a sad story about Trixie's meteoric fall from fame and Apollo Demakis had been embarrassed into taking steps to ensure that his ex-girlfriend and his daughter did not end up homeless and living apart again. An old farmhouse in the depths of the English countryside had been assigned to Trixie and Prudence for their use. Trixie might loathe country life but Prudence loved it and she had often had cause to be grateful for the security of a roof over their heads that could neither be sold nor taken from them.

Having also lived through her mother's many tumultuous affairs of the heart, Prudence believed that she cherished few illusions about men. If she had worn a romantic glow while thinking about Nikolos Angelis it could only have been the result of foolish, self-indulgent daydreams. After all, she was painfully aware that fairy stories didn't happen in real life. Rich men most often married rich women. If a rich man married a poor woman she would have some redeeming feature like stunning beauty to even the balance. But then in her unfortunate mother's case even beauty hadn't worked a miracle. In the same way gorgeous men tended to marry gorgeous women and Nikolos was drop-dead dazzling.

The girls in his set mobbed him, hung on his every word, flirted like mad with him, fought over him—in short, acted like sex-starved tarts. He could hardly avoid knowing the extent of his own pulling power. Of course, he had been spoilt by the awe, admiration and attention he commanded. A bus load of generous good fairies seemed to have blessed his privileged birth. He was highly intelligent, incredibly arrogant and impossibly proud. No more impervious to his raw, charismatic attraction than any other girl, Prudence had been wildly impressed by him as well. But what had tipped her from having a harmless fascination with his incredible looks into falling hopelessly in love was the entirely unexpected streak of stubborn gallantry that Nikolos had revealed.

On more than one occasion, Nikolos had come to Prudence's rescue when his friends decided to make her the butt of their cruel sense of humour. Why? Prudence's companion, Eirene, thoroughly resented having to take Prudence everywhere she went. The other girl's animosity had been expressed by nasty jokes and comments that targeted Prudence's lack of attraction, her weight, her cheap clothing and her apparent stupidity. Eirene's friends had soon jumped on the same bandwagon.

That Nikolos Angelis should come to her aid with his lightning-fast stabs of wit and create a distraction to deflect un-friendly attention from her had truly staggered Prudence. After all, he had still contrived to act most of the time as if she was invisible and utterly beneath his exalted notice. But that wholly disconcerting display of essential male protective-ness had touched Prudence deeply. Nikolos might be hatefully arrogant, domineering and superior, but he was also the bold, living, breathing essence of tough, unapologetic masculinity. She could not believe that he would accept the demeaning matrimonial lifebelt that Theo Demakis planned to throw in his direction.

Within forty-eight hours, when she was summoned to her grandfather's study, Prudence learnt that she was very much mistaken on that score.

'Come with me.' The older man's heavy features wore a nauseating expression of triumph. 'Nikolos Angelis is wait-ing for you in the drawing room. I met with his father and the lawyers this morning. All the essentials have been agreed. Your mother's debts will be settled and I will advance funds for a private rehabilitation programme for her. You and Nikolos will be husband and wife within the month.'

'Husband and…w-wife?' Shock ripped through Prudence in a blinding wave. Her grandfather had been right and she had been wrong; Nikolos *was* willing to marry her to save his family from impoverishment. Did he feel that he had as little choice as she had? Given the option, Prudence knew she could not turn her back on her needy mother, leaving Trixie to sink as she surely would without support and treatment. It finally dawned on her that both she and Nikolos were well and truly trapped by loyalty and good intentions and her heart sank, for, just as she was quite sure that he did not want to marry her, she was no more eager to become his un-wanted wife.

'What a very fortunate young woman you are! Don't keep your bridegroom waiting.' Smirking with derisive amusement, Theo Demakis urged his reluctant granddaughter across the hall towards the drawing room. 'Now we've caught him, don't let your prize slip the net!'

The instant Prudence entered the large, over-furnished room, she collided with shimmering golden eyes and knew beyond doubt that Nikolos had heard her grandfather's scornful taunt. Even while she tried to make herself look away, another less sensible part of her wanted to savour every aspect of his appearance. Alas, the well-cut dark suit he wore teamed with a white shirt made him look distinctly intimidating. She had never seen him in such formal clothing: he might have been dressed to attend a funeral, she thought dismally, scanning the stony impassivity of his demeanour. Nerves made her stumble over the corner of a rug and bump her hip on a small table. She felt hideously like a baby elephant penned up in a confined space.

'Oh, my goodness…sorry,' she muttered, righting the rocking table with a frantic hand.

Nikolos had noticed that before; she said sorry even when she didn't do anything wrong. He surveyed her from the floor up with rigorous thoroughness. In true Demakis style, she had not grown up but out and she barely reached the top of his chest; she was small and dumpy. She wore drab layers like an old lady: a brown skirt that almost reached her ankles, a long, loose white over-shirt, a black knee-length wrap cardigan. It was impossible to tell what lay beneath all that cloaking fabric. He imagined telling her to take it all off so that he could see exactly what he was getting. Her grandfather wouldn't object. Demakis was a vicious bastard. Even so, the older man had spelt out the grim reality that his granddaughter was in love and eager to marry the object of her affections.

'Do you have to stare at me?' Prudence breathed tautly.

'I never took the time to look at you before.' Nikolos continued to study her with unapologetic intensity. She was going to be his wife. She might as well get the message now that he would do exactly as he liked and that baklava was off the menu for the foreseeable future. She was not fat, he told himself, just a little rounded and solid. He continued to mentally score her attributes. Lots and lots of long, shiny chestnut-brown hair the colour of an English autumn. OK, a positive at last. Skin with the flush of a peach and perfect—another plus. Eyes that were the soft blue of a winter sky and full of unhappiness.

'Please…' she gasped urgently.

Nikolos saw the glimmer of tears in her strained gaze and removed his attention from her again. He had seen more than he wanted to see and he was angry with her for having so little *savoir-faire*. A Greek girl would have had refreshments served while she made polite enquiries about his family. What did she have to be unhappy about? The lack of romantic frills? What more could she ask from him? Wasn't she getting the husband she wanted? Hadn't Theo Demakis virtually *bought* her husband for her? That humiliating thought lanced through his tall, lean physique like a poisoned knife.

Prudence was trembling. She felt horribly like some slave girl on the sale block and was vaguely surprised Nikolos hadn't checked her teeth. His hard self-assurance took her equally aback for she had assumed that the situation would bring down the barriers of polite reserve between them. In the face of such odds, his forbidding cool was daunting. 'I didn't want this…if there was any other way…' Her nervous, apologetic voice ran quickly out of steam.

His handsome mouth took on a sardonic edge, for he was not impressed by her claim. 'But there isn't. We should talk about terms.'

Her long brown lashes lifted. 'Terms?' she said blankly.

'This is an arranged marriage and we're almost strangers. It will work better if we are honest with each other now.'

Prudence breathed in deeply. 'Can't we just behave like friends?'

Against the backdrop of the family lawyers still battling to hammer out a financial agreement with his mother distraught and his father wretched with guilt, that question struck Nikolos as utterly naïve. He could only think that she was as thick as a brick. 'Friends don't marry and have children. I need to know what you expect from me as a husband.'

Discomfiture at that reference to children tensed Prudence's small, taut frame. 'I know that I'm not the wife you'd have picked for yourself. I suppose we'll just learn to manage as we go along.'

'That's a recipe for chaos.'

'But you wouldn't like rules.'

His keen amber scrutiny flared in surprise at that level of perception and arrowed back to her. No, not thick as a brick, he registered, a frown of disconcertion momentarily pleating his winged ebony brows.

He reached for her hand. 'I have a ring…it belonged to my grandmother. Of course, if you don't like it, you can—'

'No…no, it's lovely; really, really lovely.' Rosy colour warmed her cheeks and rare pleasure enfolded her. The ruby and diamond ring slid onto her finger as though it belonged there. His gift of a family heirloom surprised and moved her. 'I wasn't expecting this…'

'It would be fair to say that life is currently full of the un-expected.' When Nikolos had flatly refused to buy an engagement ring, his father had persuaded him to bring the ruby. Symeon had, however, forecast that Prudence would be offended by the presentation of an unfashionable, if valuable, piece of jewellery that had belonged to someone else first.

'Thank you…' Prudence's voice was husky with emotion. She studied the ring from all angles, admiring the deep scarlet glow of the ruby and the glitter of the diamonds. That it fitted as though it had been made for her struck her as a good omen.

Discomfited by the level of her enthusiasm, Nikolos shrugged in a very masculine way and stayed silent. It was dawning on him that, apart from a shabby plastic watch, he had never seen her wear a single piece of jewellery and that it was perfectly possibly she did not own any. Suddenly he wished he had bought a proper ring for her. 'Pudding…' he breathed with uncharacteristic awkwardness. 'Do you mind if I call you that?'

'No, of course not…I've always hated the name I was born with.' The nickname that had embarrassed her suddenly acquired acceptability on his lips and seemed more in the nature of an endearing pet name. 'I'll be the best wife I can be…'

Nikolos almost groaned out loud. He knew she was dying to hear him say the same thing back on his own behalf but he would not lie to her. He was a long way from achieving an accepting state of grace, if he ever could. He didn't want to marry her. He didn't want to be married, full stop. Nor did he want a baby, he conceded with corrosive bitterness. Nothing was likely to alter those irrefutable facts.

Three short weeks later, almost lost in a frothy sea of handmade lace and expensive silken fabric, Prudence walked down the aisle on her grandfather's arm to become a wife. Although she took small, sensible steps, she was mentally floating on air and overjoyed to be marrying the man she loved. Not a single doubt clouded her optimistic outlook.

As the day moved on, however, harsh reality was destined to deliver a series of knockout blows to her rosy hopes for the future Within hours, her happiness would be destroyed and her trust shattered. When her bridegroom drank himself unconscious at the reception and had to be carried into the marital bedroom, only Theo Demakis was tactless enough to laugh. Hurt and humiliated beyond all bearing, Prudence suppressed all recollection of ever having thought that they might have had a real marriage because she was mortified by her naïvety. In spite of that common-sense attitude, the wedding night that never happened would still be the longest night of her life...

CHAPTER ONE

'I CAN'T MAKE it to your party,' Nikolos told the woman reclining on the bed, pulling on the jacket of his suit with the fluid grace that distinguished all his movements.

'Please…pretty please…' Naked but for a turquoise silk wrap, Tania Benson leapt up and curled her arms round his neck, deploying her long, rangy, supermodel body like a lethal weapon of persuasion. 'I want you to be there.'

'No strings,' Nikolos reminded her, irritated by her persistence. Their relationship was basic and not exclusive, for they often went months without contact. He only saw Tania when he was in Paris or Brussels. To complement her position in his life, he enjoyed the company of an Icelandic blonde in New York and a sultry Russian model in London.

The redhead pouted. 'I've never asked you for a favour before.'

Nikolos shrugged. She had not had to ask, because he was a very generous lover and she knew the score as well as he did.

'You couldn't make it last year either!'

'I have another engagement.' His tone was cool, clipped. He came and went as he pleased. Without explanation or apology. That had been the agreement and he had no desire for anything else. Certainly not the whole dating-type scenario of being shown off like some trophy tycoon at a celebrity party. It would also be indiscreet, since his appearance at a fashionable party was a virtual guarantee of photos and comment in the gossip columns. Once, Nikolos conceded grimly, he had been a lot less considerate about the level of public interest his way of life could attract.

Furious at that flat rejection, Tania looked sulky. 'I know what that engagement is, too…'

His dark golden eyes became semi-veiled, the hard, dynamic cast of his darkly handsome features suddenly still and impassive. 'The limo will be waiting.'

'It's *her* birthday, isn't it? Your wife's?' Tania launched at him.

His brilliant gaze bore the chill of reserve. He swept up his cashmere overcoat and moved to the door. 'I have to go—'

'I saw a photo of her in a magazine. She was wearing freaky floral Wellington boots and a woolly hat, and she was holding a rabbit… How can you prefer her to me?' Tania wailed in melodramatic disbelief.

Pale with outrage below his bronzed skin, Nikolos stayed only long enough to spell out the fact that their connection was at an end and he would not be visiting again. A stormy light in his usually cool gaze, he flung himself into the opulent limo. The floral boots had been one of the very few successful gifts he had managed to choose for his wife. How dare Tania sneer at her? He never discussed Pudding with anyone, not even his family. But the state of his marriage did awaken a good deal of curiosity. After all, he had been married for almost eight years and had lived apart from his wife for most of that period.

Time had done surprisingly little to blot out his recollection of their disastrous wedding. When he recalled his own behaviour towards the close of that day, a raw sense of guilt and insecurity wholly foreign to his forceful nature still assailed Nikolos. He rarely let himself think about it: going there was not productive. He had had to accept Pudding's refusal to even discuss what had happened that night. Her distress had silenced him as nothing else could have done. While she had been reluctant to even listen to his explanation and his apologies, he had been too proud to admit that he had no memory whatsoever of events on their wedding night. Naturally he had been afraid of what he might have said or done to her during it. Had he sunk low enough to take his angry sense of injustice out on her in bed? Had he been rough?

Those all too male apprehensions still haunted Nikolos in low moments and sent a cold stab of foreboding through him, for he knew his own flaws only too well. He had the devil's own temper. He was very hard and had often in recent years been called cold, callous and cruel. Dealing with Theo Demakis, he had had to be all of those things many times over. Had he not been strong and ruthless, he would still have been dependent on his father-in-law's goodwill. Instead he had paid back the amount incurred by the debts Theo had settled, left his family secure and bought his independence back. He had then picked the optimum right moment to walk away from Demakis International with Theo's agreement, if not his blessing.

In truth there were very few people in the world that Nikolos cared about. While willing to do his utmost to help those precious few, he remained utterly indifferent to the plight of everyone else. Around Prudence, however, he made a major effort to be a softer, gentler and more compassionate guy than he could ever be in real life. Her temperament was the polar opposite of his, for she was neither aggressive nor cunning. Indeed, human evil always shocked Pudding, who was full of decent scruples and lived life entirely by the rules. Unselfish, kind and endlessly sympathetic, she had trained as a veterinary nurse and now devoted all her spare time to the needs of the animals in the sanctuary she ran. From behind the scenes, Nikolos tried to protect her from those who would have taken advantage of her trusting nature. Of course, he cared about her: she was his wife. Possibly, it would soon be time for him to bring an end to their separate lives and settle down into being married, Nikolos conceded lazily.

Prudence woke up at six on the morning of her birthday and, as always, let her gaze fall on the photograph of Nikolos that held pride of place by her bed: black hair tousled by the rain, stunning dark eyes gleaming, perfect white teeth dazzling against his bronzed skin as he laughed and mopped himself dry in her homely kitchen. It had been taken the previous year on one of his flying visits. She had entire albums and scrap-books filled with photos, tabloid cuttings and memorabilia about him. For so long she had acted like a schoolgirl running a one-woman secret fan club.

Even though she saw him only a handful of times a year, Nikolos had been the centre of her world. His sexy drawl on the phone and the nurse he had insisted on hiring had lifted her sagging spirits when times were tough during her mother's long, slow decline and after her death the previous year. She had enjoyed days out in London when he would meet her for lunch and afterwards give her the official tour of his latest new office building or his most recent business ac-quisition. Although she had never lived with him as his wife, she was proud that she had had the maturity to overcome the disillusionment of their wedding night and win his trust as a friend.

It was really only after Trixie had died that Prudence had

had the time to think about her own needs and what was best for her, and she had almost immediately boxed up the albums and put them away. Nourishing a morbid interest in Nik's taste in other women and cherishing a girlish flame of unrequited love was doing her no favours. Having finally come to terms with those facts, she had sunk her energy into the animal sanctuary. She had got over Nik and her longings for him. That was an achievement of which she was immensely proud. Slowly but surely she had also begun to understand what would really make her happy. To be truly, madly happy, she had decided, she needed a child on whom she could heap all the love she had to give. And very fortunately for her, she thought wryly, medical science meant that she was not dependent on Nik to make her dream of motherhood come true.

Feeling buoyant at the very idea of attaining her dream of eventually becoming a mother, Prudence reached for the photo of Nik, opened the drawer in the bedside cabinet and carefully put it away. Before she could even contemplate having a child, she had to get a divorce from Nik and she was ready to take that step. Once they were divorced, however, Nik would vanish from her life, for she was convinced that he only maintained regular contact with her out of a sense of duty and responsibility. Some day soon, therefore, she would never lay eyes on him again…

An unexpected knock on the bedroom door jolted Prudence out of her disturbing thoughts. Dottie, a rotund little dynamo of a woman in her fifties, appeared with a broad smile and a breakfast tray.

'Dottie…my goodness, you shouldn't have!'

'After everything that you've done for Sam and me, I don't want to hear another word. It's your birthday. Enjoy! We'll feed the animals today—'

'No, no way! Leo's coming and the vet's due later. You'll

have plenty to do while I'm out. Anyway, breakfast is more than sufficient.'

But of course Dottie and her husband, Sam, the tenants of the tiny cottage attached to the end wall of the farmhouse, had a card and a gift for her as well. Prudence embarked on the morning feeding routine later than she usually did.

'So…this is the big day,' Leo commented when he arrived to help her. 'Ready for blast-off?'

'Stop teasing me.' Prudence threw the tall, fair-haired teacher a cheerful look of reproach as she doled out bran mash for a pair of elderly donkeys. The sanctuary had a rota of willing helpers but Leo Burleigh was the most knowledgeable and regular. He lived only a field away and in recent years had become her closest friend. 'Nik won't bat an eyelash when I tell him my plans. He's unshockable—'

'With regard to his own freedom of choice,' Leo slotted in wryly. 'But I'll be surprised if he takes the same liberal view of his wife's lifestyle—'

'For goodness' sake, don't call me *that*.' Prudence tossed some carrot and apple into the mash before moving on to the next shed to attend to an orphaned fox cub that had been brought in. 'I'm not and I have never been Nik's wife—'

'Yet he refers to you as his wife in interviews—'

'That's just because journalists ask him stupid, nosy questions and he's forced to pretend—'

'Maybe he's not pretending. It could be that he's very much an old-style, unreconstructed and thoroughly sexist Greek tycoon—'

'Nik's not an old-style anything!'

'Isn't he? Some would say that accepting an arranged marriage for family reasons was incredibly medieval but he did it. He also runs a stable of mistresses but still has no problem regarding you as his wife—'

'Nik looks on me as a friend but I suspect that a few years back…' Prudence ducked her head down, wishing Leo hadn't mentioned the mistresses as her tummy always turned queasy when anyone referred to that subject. '…well, back then he had a fair idea of my feelings for him. I think that's why he didn't ask for a divorce the minute he was free to walk out of Demakis International.'

'You certainly took the heat off Nik Angelis there,' Leo mused, watching her take care of the cub with the minimum of fuss. 'Didn't your grandfather blame you for walking out on your marriage to come back to England and look after your mother?'

'By that stage I don't really think my grandfather gave two hoots what I did,' Prudence countered wryly.

Just when Theo Demakis had been in the act of divorcing his estranged wife that same year, the lady had announced that she was pregnant. Jubilant at having fathered his own child, her grandfather had lost interest in the idea of Nik and Prudence providing the next generation. Sadly, however, the story had recently reached a most unhappy conclusion when DNA testing had revealed that Theo's son and heir was not his child after all. A very bitter divorce had taken place and the older man's response had been anything but gracious when Prudence had written in all sincerity to offer her sympathy.

'But as your husband, Nik may well have a different perspective on your current plans,' Leo warned her. 'Just watch how you break the news about the sperm bank…'

Prudence turned an uncomfortable pink. 'I wasn't planning to mention that just yet.'

Nik was not due until one. But a couple who had adopted a dog from the sanctuary called back for a visit and by the time they departed Prudence was running exceedingly late. She pulled on the long grey skirt and a blouse and jacket that she currently reserved for special occasions and began applying polish to her short nails in a rush. When she dropped the brush and smeared peach polish over her blouse and skirt, she could've screamed. The clattering whap-whap of Nik's helicopter was already sounding overhead. Raking through a wardrobe that offered no formal alternatives, she dragged out a flouncy cerise sun dress that she kept for the garden and hauled it on. It fell to her ankles but bared her shoulders and most of her arms. Grimacing at her reflection, she unfolded a lilac pashmina and wrapped it round her as tightly and thoroughly as if she was facing a blizzard.

She liked to cover up and hated wearing anything that might draw attention to her full figure. Her mother had once wept inconsolably in her disappointment at having an only child who had failed to inherit her slender blonde beauty. Having accepted that she was homely, Prudence gave very little thought to her appearance. She was five feet two inches tall with a big bosom and generous hips. Although the adolescent plumpness she had suffered had mercifully melted away as she left the teenage years behind, she knew that she had no hope of ever attaining the tall, skinny, long-legged look of her youthful fantasies.

The helicopter landed in the paddock next to the house. Nik, immaculate in his designer-cut charcoal-grey suit, sprang out and headed for the front door. A man emerged from the barn toting a bale of hay. The two men exchanged nods. Nik hit the doorbell. Just when he was about to try the back door instead, Prudence appeared, breathless and flushed. 'Nikolos…'

'Pudding…' Nik bent down to kiss her on both cheeks. Her chestnut-brown hair swung forward, her delicate floral scent filling his nostrils. He stepped back from her again, feeling oddly awkward with her for the first time in years. He wondered if he should mention that pashminas were usually draped rather than tied and decided not to bother.

Her soft blue gaze whipped over him and then off him again. As always he dazzled her. Sunshine gleamed over his short, luxuriant black hair, highlighting his superb classical bone structure and dark, deep-set golden eyes. He was so incredibly tall and well-built. She felt a little breathless and that annoyed her. She could not bear to feel any response to Nik. Friendship was asexual and she had accepted that a long time ago.

'Oh, my goodness, I forgot to tell Leo something…excuse me,' Prudence gasped, hurrying across the yard in pursuit of the man whom Nik had seen earlier.

Leo? But Leo was an old guy, wasn't he? The frequency with which she mentioned that name had made it familiar to Nik. He rested his shrewd scrutiny on the handsome blond man. He tensed when Prudence rested her hand on the guy's arm in a revealing gesture of ease and trust and laughed at something he said. A frown line drew Nik's well-shaped ebony brows together. Who the hell was this joker? Prudence could be dangerously naïve.

'Who was that?' Nik enquired on the way back to the helicopter.

'Leo… My word, I forgot you hadn't met each other! I should have introduced you—'

'Never mind that now. I understood that Leo was about seventy-five…'

'That was his father, Leo senior. He was a lovely old man. He used to call in every day.' Prudence loosed a regretful sigh.

'I remember you mentioning it…so what happened to the lovely old man?'

'He died about eighteen months ago.'

'You seem very friendly with his son.'

'I ought to be…he's been living practically next door for ages and he's probably my closest friend on this planet! I'm very fond of him,' Prudence confided without hesitation.

Nik's lean, strong face clenched. Of course, there was nothing going on; he knew that. Prudence wasn't the type. She was very honest and downright prudish. She was more interested in animal welfare and her garden than in men. With the exception of himself, of course. On the other hand, Nik had never believed that true platonic friendship was possible between men and women and he was suddenly conscious that she had been alone for a long time.

The helicopter delivered them to an exclusive country-house hotel. A table embellished with exquisite china, crystal and candles awaited them in a private room. French windows stood open on a stone balcony that overlooked the river. Having chosen her meal, Prudence wandered outside with a glass of orange juice to take in the view of the lush countryside. Too warm in the sunlight, she untied her wrap. Nik always made such an occasion of their meetings. She suppressed a pang of sadness, for she knew that she would really miss his presence in her life. But then, making things special for a woman came easily to Nikolos Angelis. Her soft eyes hardened to a surprisingly steely hue. When a guy kept three mistresses he had loads of opportunities to practise his womanising charm.

Nikolos strolled out to join her. 'Happy birthday.'

'Let's not mind that now. I've something important to say to you and I'd just as soon say it before we sit down to eat.' Prudence lifted her chin and smiled just a touch woodenly. 'We got married because it was the practical thing to do…'

Nik was startled, for their conversations always remained

safely rooted in the uncontroversial present. He stilled. 'That's not how I would put it—'

'Does it matter how I put it?' Prudence wrinkled her nose. 'I only want to say that I think it's time we divorced.'

The sudden silence seemed to rush like the unearthly quiet before a storm in Prudence's ears.

'Divorce?' Nik studied her with fiercely narrowed dark eyes. 'What is this? Where is this nonsense coming from?'

Disconcerted in turn, Prudence blinked. 'I don't understand. Nonsense…how is it nonsense?'

'In my family we don't do divorce.'

'Don't you?' Unimpressed, Prudence raised a brow. 'Well, thank goodness I'm not part of your family!'

Nik lounged back against the balustrade and surveyed her steadily. 'You are angry with me…very angry.'

'Anger would be too strong a word. I'm irritated. You're making a quite unnecessary big deal out of something trivial—'

'Since when was marriage a trivial matter?'

Although Nik was laying himself wide open for a counterattack, Prudence valiantly resisted the temptation. 'I don't think I could comment on that when we've never had a normal marriage. Whatever, I would like a divorce now.'

Shimmering dark golden eyes lit on her like torches. 'Why?'

The atmosphere was leaping and jumping with hostile vibrations. Thinking about her maternal ambitions, Prudence squirmed. In the mood he was in she was not prepared to bare her soul to him. 'I don't need to give you a reason—'

'Yes, you do.' His accent raked round the edges of her response, the intonation grim and intimidating.

Nik had never spoken to Prudence like that before and she resented it very much. 'No, I don't.'

Without warning, Nik flung up lean brown hands in an expansive gesture of frustration and reproof that was explosively Greek. 'What's come over you? Where is all this coming from?'

Soft pink mouth compressed, Prudence shrugged and turned away in a defensive movement to gaze out over the fast-flowing river. 'Don't talk down to me like I'm stupid—'

'I have not done that.'

'That's exactly what you're doing!'

Nik prided himself on his control over his temper. He had never dreamt that Pudding, of all people, would push him to the brink of losing it. He surveyed her with fulminating force. Without her awareness the pashmina had slid down her arms, baring her smooth, rounded shoulders and the creamy swell of her full breasts. Nik stared. He could not help staring, for he had not seen that much of her since the neckline of her wedding gown had showcased her ample curves and filled him with an instant lust that almost embarrassed him in the church. She had the kind of opulent bosom popularised by forties film stars in tight sweaters. It was many years since he had allowed himself to recall that fact. Suddenly he was having trouble concentrating. 'I bring you here in all good faith to celebrate your birthday and out of nowhere you make—'

'A perfectly reasonable suggestion that, since the emergency is long since over, we dissolve the legal connection between us!' Prudence completed heatedly.

'And I asked…perfectly reasonably…why?'

Her chin came up, her blue eyes bright with defiance. 'That's none of your business.'

Nik could not credit what he was hearing. 'I insist…'

A little scarlet devil literally leapt up in the invigorating surge of Prudence's anger. If he wanted the whole truth and nothing but the truth she would give it to him. 'All right…'

'Let's eat while we talk.' Nik urged her back indoors to where the first course awaited them.

Prudence sat down. Even in that short space of time her temper was fading and she was shaken by the hostility in the air, not to mention her own unfamiliar desire to fight with him. For goodness' sake, she was hugely fond of Nik. There was no sense in destroying their friendship by trying to score points. An apologetic light in her soft blue eyes, she forced a smile back on her tense mouth and speared a juicy cube of melon. 'I can't believe we're arguing.'

'Believe it.' Bereft of an appetite for food, Nik rested back in his seat in an attitude of highly deceptive indolence. His cutting-edge logic had already led him to draw a conclusion that shook him to his core. There was another man in her life; there *had* to be. For what other reason would she suddenly demand a divorce?

Prudence stole a glance at him from below her eyelashes. His remarkable eyes were smouldering like the stormy heart of a fire, eyes the colour of amber and precious gold that had haunted her thoughts for *far* too long, she conceded guiltily. Breaking free, breaking the final bond was the healthy thing to do. Lingering on the edge of his life was pitiful, she reminded herself.

'But there's no need whatsoever for this bad feeling,' she murmured quietly. 'I'm so fond of you…'

'You're also fond of cats, dogs, foxes, badgers, donkeys, horses…in fact, all the members of the animal kingdom…and of most of the people you meet.'

The vein of derisive dismissal in that response made Prudence redden. 'I thought you'd want a divorce, too. I don't see the problem unless it's because I came up with the idea first. It's not as if we've ever been married like other people—'

Nikolos levelled brooding eyes on her. 'Whose choice was that?'

Her smooth brow furrowed. 'I beg your pardon?'

'I asked you whose choice it was that we ended up with a marriage that never got off the starting blocks.'

Her sense of perplexity deepened. 'I always thought it was a mutual thing—'

'Did you really?' His rich, dark drawl was so quiet she actually leant forward to hear him, her whole attention welded to his lean, strong face. 'Yet you're the one who moved out of my bedroom. You're the one who had hysterics when I tried to kiss you. You're the one who took the first excuse available to leave Greece and stay away.'

It was Prudence's turn to disbelieve the evidence of her own ears. Her eyes had opened very wide. 'Er—you're complaining?'

'I was in no position to complain, was I?' Nik breathed, tight-mouthed.

Prudence had no idea what he was driving at and she lacked the ability to listen and learn, for she did not want to relive the painful period of unhappiness she had endured before she bit the bullet and left Greece. Her face felt all tight and her tummy muscles were taut with stress. 'Well, I hardly think you were likely to complain, Nik. In fact, I think it's very hypocritical of you to make comments of that nature—'

'Is that a fact?'

'Yes, it is a fact. Honestly, I don't understand why you're acting like this,' Prudence condemned shakily, pushing her chair back from the table in a sudden movement. 'After all, I know you must have been hugely relieved when Trixie's illness gave me a very solid reason to get back out of your life again!'

'That is not true,' Nik shot back.

Prudence was flushed and trembling. When it came to talking about anything that touched on the hurt and humiliation of their marriage, she reached the edge of her control very fast. 'I'm sorry,' she said fiercely. 'But that's not a very convincing protest from a guy who got himself blind drunk so that he could successfully avoid having to consummate our marriage!'

For an instant, Nik sat as though he had been turned to stone. Then with equal rapidity he sprang upright, took a pace forward and stood over her, six feet three inches of uncompromising, aggressive masculinity. His darkly handsome features were forbidding. 'Say that again…' he urged thickly.

'I don't think so.' Instinct made Prudence scramble up and go straight into retreat.

'You said that I successfully avoided…consummating our marriage…'

Eggs could have fried on Prudence's hot cheeks. She could not believe that, eight years after the event, she had got so upset that she had sunk to the level of actually throwing that humiliating fact at him.

Scorching dark golden eyes locked to her discomfited face. 'Are you saying that nothing happened between us on our wedding night? Nothing…*at all*?'

'I hardly think that can be news to you,' Prudence muttered, ducking her head down, talking to her toes.

Rage roared through Nik's lean, powerful frame like a flaming fireball. He felt light-headed with the force of it. In all his life he could never recall being so angry. Yet at the same time what he had just found out banished the dark spectre of guilt that had dogged him for so many years. He had not touched her in anger or in desire on their wedding night. He felt amazingly liberated by that knowledge. With a swift jerk of his head he dismissed the waiter entering with a laden trolley. Closing his hand over Prudence's, he pulled her out of the room in his imperious wake. An unexpected emergency, he told the hotel manager. His bodyguards bringing up the rear and depriving them of privacy, he headed back out to the helicopter, still without offering Prudence a word of explanation.

What's happening? Where are we going? What about lunch? Why are you acting like this? All those questions flashed through her head but caution kept her silent. Had he just flipped at the reminder that their wedding night had been the non-event of the decade? But it didn't fit his character; the Nikolos Angelis she had always known was a lot cooler than that.

Back at the farmhouse, Nik thrust wide the front door and strode into the sitting room. His stunning eyes welded to her in a blaze of wrath. 'Do you realise that for eight years I've been blaming myself for something that never happened?'

Prudence gazed back at him, her brow furrowed with confusion. 'I don't know what you're talking about. What have you been blaming yourself for?'

Nik strode forward, dominating the room with the strength of his sheer presence and size. 'When I woke up the morning after our wedding, I was naked—'

'Your friends did that—'

'The bed had been stripped and remade…'

'You asked me for a drink of water and I spilt it all over the bed, so I changed it.' Prudence was frowning. 'Are you saying you were too drunk that night to remember anything the next day?'

'It's still a blank. I don't remember the evening part of the reception or anything until late the next morning. I had a complete blackout… I told you that at the time.'

Prudence looked away, tension thrumming through her. The room felt suffocatingly warm and she pulled open the patio door to let cooler air flow in from the terrace outside. 'I assumed that was just an excuse, something you were just saying to cover up—'

'Why would I lie?' Nik incised curtly.

She heaved a rueful sigh. 'Because people do when they've taken too much alcohol—'

'By all accounts your mother had a problem telling the truth sober *or* under the influence. So don't compare us.'

'You're not being fair to her when you say that.' But Prudence was painfully aware that Nik and her mother had mixed like oil and water. Trixie had bitterly resented her daughter's refusal to profit from her marriage into the wealthy Angelis clan and accept an allowance from Nik. Her mother's acid comments when Nik visited had led Prudence to suggest that she see Nik in London instead.

Nik rested grim, dark golden eyes on her. 'I wasn't lying to you when I said I had a blackout—'

'That may be the case,' Prudence conceded reluctantly. 'But I didn't know you well enough then to be able to tell the difference.'

His burning anger undimmed, Nikolos stepped back from her and swung away, tension emanating from him in waves. 'The day after our wedding you shrank away from me,' he breathed thickly. 'You wouldn't meet my eyes. You couldn't even bear me to touch your hand—'

'I just don't want to talk about this!' Prudence exclaimed, emotion whipping up a storm inside her because she was already recalling her anguished sense of rejection that day. She had learned to live with it but she still despised herself for the love that had cost her so dear.

Nik swung back to her, astonishingly fast and light on his feet for all his size. 'Tough,' he pronounced. 'You're going to talk about it. I'm not tiptoeing round your strait-laced notions of sexual propriety this time around.'

Utterly off-balanced by his aggressive stance and his hostility, Prudence drew in a quivering breath. 'I would suggest that the practice of propriety is not one of your skills—'

'You throw it up like a barrier between us.' Nik strolled almost lazily round her, brilliant dark eyes watching the way sunshine lit up the lighter streaks of gold and amber in her hair while he wondered when he had last seen hair that natural and abundant. 'But I won't tolerate that again—'

Oddly uneasy with the way he was watching her, Prudence was standing as straight and stiff as a board. 'I don't want to discuss—'

'What about what I want and need?' Nik shot back at her, hard as a diamond cutting through steel. 'You still speak as if I chose to get drunk that night. My drink was spiked—'

'So you said at the time.' Prudence was keen to get the discussion over with, since it seemed there was no hope of silencing him.

Nik bit out an incredulous laugh. 'You didn't believe that either, did you?'

'No, I didn't.'

'But it was the truth. Someone spiked my drink with a drug. I can only believe it was someone's idea of a joke but it wasn't very funny for either of us,' Nik pronounced harshly. 'It ruined our wedding, humiliated me and made trouble between us.'

Even though Prudence was now prepared to accept that he had been telling the truth, she turned her head away. She was very pale. All the wedding guests had known why Nik was marrying her and he had come in a good deal of sympathy. As the outsider and the grandchild of an unpopular man, she had been despised. But had drugging Nik into a state of unconsciousness on his wedding night been intended as a joke?

Or as a favour to him? Certainly, Nik had been in no condition to act the bridegroom. Some might well have assumed that that would be a welcome escape from an unpleasant task when the bride was plain and unattractive. She was convinced that the stifled sniggers of amusement that she had heard that night would live with her to her dying day.

'I was more humiliated than you were,' she muttered in a rush, swallowing hard, but it was no use: she just could not keep the tears from hitting the backs of her eyes and threatening to overflow.

In a movement that took Nik by surprise she spun round and walked hurriedly out into the garden. She came to a halt below the apple trees and dragged in a great gulp of fresh air, fighting for her composure.

'How do you make that out?'

Startled, Prudence whirled round. Nik was on the terrace. Raw pain sliced through her as she focused on his lean, devastatingly handsome features. 'When you had to marry me, your family and your friends felt *so* sorry for you,' she remembered jaggedly. 'Nobody was that surprised when it looked like you'd got plastered at the prospect of having to sleep with me!'

A dull edge of colour seared a faint line along the angular slant of his proud, chiselled cheekbones. He had not known she thought so little of herself and it disturbed him. 'You can't have thought that…. How could you make such a drama out of nothing?'

'It wasn't nothing.' Bitterly regretting her candour, Prudence bent her head and went back indoors. She could not stay still. Time was threatening to take her back where she didn't want to go and she saw no advantage to reliving her agonies as a lovelorn teenager whose dream wedding had descended into pure gothic tragedy.

'Is the humiliation you believe you suffered the reason you refused to discuss what happened that night?'

'You're so persistent.'

'And you're surprised?' Nik dealt her a scorching appraisal from his mesmerising eyes, his beautiful mouth a bleak line. 'I didn't know what had happened and you wouldn't tell me, so I assumed the worst. I wasn't in control after I took that drink…the way you behaved and reacted the next day, I thought I must have been rough—'

'Rough?'

'In bed…that I'd hurt you, offended you, forced you to do something you didn't want to do, *whatever*!' Nik ground out with raking impatience and distaste. 'It never once occurred to me that we might not have made love at all.'

Prudence did not know where to look. Her face was hot and pink. 'In the condition you were in, I wouldn't have let you touch me—'

'But I'm a whole lot bigger and stronger than you are,' Nik said darkly. 'You were a virgin and I was in no state to consider that. When you refused to look at me the following morning, I felt like a rapist!'

Freezing in consternation, Prudence gave him an aghast glance. 'Oh, no…surely not?'

Shimmering golden eyes lanced into hers. 'What else was I to believe? Obviously I'd messed up badly. When I tried to kiss you, you began sobbing and you took off like a bullet out of a gun and locked yourself in the bedroom next door…'

Prudence sucked in a fracturing breath. She was beginning to see how misleading her behaviour must have been from his point of view and feel guilty. Unfortunately, she did not want the dialogue he was making it impossible for her to avoid. Yet if he did not remember that night, it was only right that she should fill in the blanks.

'Before you passed out at the reception, you went missing and I made it my mission to find you. You were with Cassia Morikis,' she framed in a flat tone that carried not a shade of human expression.

Nik frowned, ebony brows pleating. 'That part of the evening is not a blank. I was OK at that point because I remember it well. Cassia was upset. I took her out of the function room because I didn't want a scene that would have embarrassed a lot of people.'

Prudence chewed the soft underside of her lower lip. She felt that she should have known that he would manage to put an entirely different spin on that episode. When it came to self-defence he moved faster than the speed of light. 'When I saw you, you were wrapped round each other like Romeo and Juliet and it didn't look quite so innocent.'

'Why wouldn't you talk about this when it happened?' Nik suddenly demanded angrily. 'Take it from me, it was innocent—'

'You were kissing her!' Prudence yelled at him, ditching her façade of waspish composure with a vengeance.

Nik held her accusing gaze with level, challenging cool while thinking about what a very luscious, sexy mouth she had. 'She was crying and she kissed me…I pushed her away—'

'Of course, I was long gone by that stage…and I really don't care now anyway,' Prudence delivered between compressed lips, twin spots of high colour illuminating her cheekbones. 'All I want from you now is a divorce.'

'Forget it…you're an Angelis; you're my wife. This entire conversation is offensive—'

'No, it's not.' Her blue eyes were dark with growing emotion. 'Offensive is you thinking that you have the right to tell me I can't have a divorce.'

Nik squared broad shoulders that were sheathed in the finest suiting available, breathed in deep and released a slow, measured hiss. 'Don't you think that we should give marriage a trial *before* we start talking about a divorce?'

CHAPTER TWO

A FALLING FEATHER would have sounded like a giant rock in
the silence that followed that question.

Shattered, Prudence opened her mouth and shut it again,
discovering that Nik's gaze was welded to her full lips. She
flushed, wondering why he was staring. She studied him with
a frown because she didn't trust her own hearing. He could
surely not have said what she thought he had just said? And
if he *had* spoken those words, no doubt she had somehow misunderstood his meaning.

Aware that his legendary skills as a negotiator had let him
down badly, Nik attempted to recoup. 'Think about this sen-
sibly. Eight years ago, we were kids. So we did what we had
to do and went through the motions and then we parted. We
didn't even try living together. But we're older and wiser
now.'

Prudence felt as if a rocket was about to fire off inside her;
containing the shockwaves was almost more than she could
handle. She shut her eyes tight. What was the matter with him?
Eight years on, eight years after breaking her heart into a million pieces with his essential indifference, he was suggesting
trying out marriage like a new pair of shoes. She wanted to
scream—but not before she strangled him for daring to offer

what she had once most craved, before she had finally got up the strength to break away. She thought of the contents of the wooden chest by the wall behind him and her fast-beating heart steadied and almost stilled as the old anguish tore at her. Not tall enough, not thin enough, not pretty enough for a guy so good-looking he turned male and female heads in the street.

'No, thanks,' Prudence said as if he had offered her a drink she didn't want.

Shock slivered through Nikolos, his golden eyes darkening. He could not credit that instant refusal. She was winding him up, he thought forbiddingly. In the back of his mind he had always known that he would settle down with her. Eventually. He had never doubted it, never really even needed to think about it. He had known she would wait for him, wait with the steady, strong patience of the intelligent woman that she was until *he* was ready to make that commitment.

'Think about what you're saying,' Nik urged huskily. 'This is you, this is me and we're already married—'

'Only on paper—'

'But we could make it real,' Nik drawled softly, the dark timbre of his accented intonation shimmying down her taut spinal cord like a dangerous-weather warning.

Prudence worked very hard at blanking him out. Goodness knew, she had had plenty of practice resisting Nik's intense charisma. Once a stray smile or even the hint of warmth in his gaze had made her silly heart race. But not any more, she reminded herself fiercely.

'I don't want to make it real.'

Nik reached for her with sure, steady hands and she let him ease her closer. Her heart was pounding behind her ribcage. Her brain was telling her to back away, laugh it off and extricate herself with style. There was just one problem: she didn't want to. A little voice had swum up from her subconscious to tell her that it was all right and perfectly acceptable to be curious about how it would feel if he held her close.

'I may be no good at the romantic angle…but I excel in other fields,' Nik purred.

'You're very modest.' She was so tense, so wound up with fizzing expectation that she could hardly breathe. In the grip of intense confusion, she was no longer thinking. In fact she was luxuriating in the touch of the long brown fingers smoothing across her cheek to spear into her hair and tip up her face for the raking inspection of his stunning golden eyes.

'Humility doesn't win battles.' He lowered his arrogant dark head. 'If you run away this time, I'll come after you…'

A tight little knot had formed in her tummy. She pressed her thighs tightly together. The peaks of her breasts felt incredibly sensitive, the rosy tips distended and tingling. Warm colour mantled her cheeks. Just when she was on the brink of grabbing him, he brought his marauding masculine mouth down on hers. It felt impossibly intimate and incredibly good. She clutched at his jacket to stay upright. *Thud-thud-thud* went her heartbeat. The invasion of his tongue beyond the tender fullness of her lips pierced her with a deep, aching longing that made her shiver. She wanted more. Her body was like a spring wound up too tight. She wanted to drown in the sweet, wicked pleasure he offered and forget her pride. But as he pulled her closer she knocked her heel on the wooden chest by the wall and cold shame engulfed her as she recognised her hunger and her weakness for what they were.

Tearing herself free of his hold, she staggered away a couple of steps and struggled to calm herself, while attempting to ignore the shrieking sensation of loss tugging at her nerve-endings.

Breathing heavily, Nik resisted an urge to haul her back to him like a caveman. 'What's wrong?'

Mortified by her behaviour, she could not stand to look at him. What was wrong was encapsulated in the contents of the chest by the wall, she reflected painfully. She wondered if he had registered that her response had hit earthquake scale and that her legs were still threatening to buckle. 'I shouldn't have let that happen—'

'Why not?'

'Because I want a divorce.'

'Why?' Nik prompted, swift as a panther about to pounce. 'Is there another man in your life?'

Astonishment almost made Prudence laugh out loud at that question. Mentally she was in a total spin: his suggestion that they make their marriage real had already shattered her with its sheer unexpectedness. The kiss, brief as it had been, had been overkill for her sorely taxed nerves. 'If there was, it would be none of your business—'

'*Theos*…of course it would be my business!' Nik launched at her, dropping the velvet-smooth approach with a vengeance.

It was the provocation Prudence needed. Stalking past him, she wrenched up the lid of the chest and bent down to lift out a haphazard bundle of photograph albums and scrapbooks. She turned round and clumsily dumped them right at his feet. 'No…the women between those pages are your business… I'm not and I never will be!'

An electrifying silence fell.

'What is this?' Nik swept up a scrapbook. He didn't want to open it. But cowardice was not his way and he did so. His arrested attention was claimed by tabloid cuttings, magazine articles and picture after picture of him with other women. He felt sick. 'You put this together?'

Prudence folded her arms in a defensive stance. 'It was wonderful aversion therapy.'

'But we weren't living together. We have never lived together as man and wife,' Nik countered in a fast-footed and healthy recovery that she could only regard as magnificent, surrounded as he was by all the undeniable evidence of his notorious reputation as a womaniser. 'But if I had you, I wouldn't need those kinds of amusements any more.'

Amusements? Women as toys, entertaining distractions for the lighter moments of life. Leo had been right and she had been ingloriously wrong: Nik *was* an old-style Greek tycoon. An unrepentant womaniser with double standards. It was typical that he should think that she would only want a divorce because she had met someone else. Perhaps honesty was the best policy.

With her emotions all over the place and her lips still tingling from the hard heat of his, Prudence was eager to gloss over the animosity in the air and smooth things back to normal. 'There is nobody else involved in this. I wasn't going to tell you at this point but I have made certain plans and I can't go ahead with them until we're divorced.'

'What sort of plans?'

'I want to…' she hesitated and then pressed doggedly on, '…I want to have a baby.'

The tall, dark Greek went as still as a statue. 'With whom?'

'By myself. It's not that unusual… I'll go to a sperm bank,' Prudence explained in a small, reluctant voice. 'And yes, I *have* thought very deeply about this.'

For a count of thirty seconds Nik stared at her with brooding force, his golden eyes burning hot as the heart of a fire. 'Over my dead body…and I mean that literally. That has to be the most disgusting idea that I've ever heard and I don't want to hear it again. It's freaky—'

'It is not freaky… There's nothing wrong with me wanting a child! It's the most normal thing in the world. I'm twenty-seven—'

'So? You can have one the normal way…but not that way.'
Pale beneath his bronzed skin, his fabulous, sculpted bone
structure prominent, Nik could not restrain a shudder. 'I suppose I could agree to a baby as well. Anything has to be better than a divorce and impregnation of my wife by a test-tube.'

Rigid with mortification and anger at his scornful and dis-
missive reaction, and outraged at his offer of that grudging
concession on the child front, Prudence said tightly, 'I think
you should leave—'

'Pudding—'

'I used to think there was something cute about you calling me that…I've changed my mind.'

In a sudden movement that caught her unawares, Nik
reached for her hands. 'No, I'm not leaving. I can't let this
happen. This is not how we are together.'

Her throat thickened and closed over. She nodded in vig-
orous agreement, not trusting herself to speak.

'This is not how it was meant to be between us,' Nik in-
toned, almost crushing the life from her fingers.

Moisture shone in her eyes and slid down her cheeks. Nik
groaned out loud. 'Don't…'

She gulped. 'I'm sorry…go!'

'No…' Nik lowered his handsome dark head to kiss the
tear from her smooth cheek. She had the scent of a peach:
warm and ripe and ready to eat. For a fraction of a second he
hesitated and then, recognising his moment, he went for it
with all the ruthless, single-minded purpose which his business competitors feared.

Astonishment shrilled through Prudence when Nik captured her lips with a hungry urgency that rocked her down to
her toes. Bemused, she began to pull away but he wound her
hair round his fingers, tipped her head back and traced a path
across her face with kisses as light and tantalising as butter-

flies. She liked it. Without meaning to, she shut her eyes and let her head fall back, extending her throat. He took instant advantage of that new expanse of territory. His mouth probed a tender spot below her ear and her pulses all leapt in concert. She gasped and shivered violently, her legs suddenly behaving like bendy twigs.

'Still want me to leave?' Nik asked soft and low.

In answer, Prudence gripped the lapels of his suit jacket and stretched up, wanting his mouth on hers again so badly she could taste it. He kissed her with a slow, sensual thoroughness that turned her bones to liquid and yet still filled her with screaming impatience. Her hands swept up over his shoulders, rejoicing in the strength of his powerful frame while her fingertips flirted with the luxuriant black hair brushing his shirt collar. She shifted against him and he caught her to him with a sensual growl low in his throat, his hands splaying across the curve of her hips to press her into energising contact with his bold arousal.

Her initial shock was followed by a giddy mixture of shy satisfaction and sudden triumph: Nik wanted her. Nik *could* find her attractive and worthy of desire. No man could fake his physical response to a woman. That knowledge filled her with a highly feminine sense of joyful achievement. He hoisted her up into his arms with a brute strength that thrilled her to the marrow. 'You make me very hot,' he whispered thickly, letting the tip of his tongue slide between her lips in a single lancing foray that set her every nerve-ending on fire.

Nik carried her into the bedroom and sank down on the bed with her. His lean, bronzed profile intent, he tugged loose the tantalising strings that shaped the neckline of her dress and buried his mouth hungrily in the deep cleavage formed by her lace-edged bra. A stifled sob of pent-up response was wrenched from Prudence. A heavy pulse of need had started to pound in her pelvis. She leant back into the support of his arm, her fingers spearing into the ebony depths of his hair. He flipped loose the hooks holding the satin cups in place, letting her firm, full breasts spill free.

'You are magnificent,' Nik told her raggedly, surveying the pouting silken swells with reverent appreciation and capturing the hands that she instinctively raised to cover herself from him. 'No, don't you dare try to hide yourself.'

Embarrassment and gratification at his response made her acquiesce. He massaged the stiff, rosy crests that crowned the creamy mounds of her breasts and she ran out of breath all at once. All of a sudden every part of her was taut and deliciously sensitised. Lowering his proud dark head, he used his mouth on the distended buds. A helpless moan broke from her, for the coil of heat unfurling low in her tummy merely intensified the tormenting ache between her thighs.

'Nik…' she gasped, amazed by the surging tide of sensation engulfing her inexperienced body.

'I know. I feel it, too.' Springing upright, he laid her down on the bed. He peeled off his jacket and let it fall where he stood. Smouldering dark golden eyes fixed to her, he yanked loose his tie and unbuttoned his shirt, revealing a muscular, bronzed wedge of chest ornamented with crispy black whorls of hair. 'We should have done this a long, long time ago.'

Her soft blue gaze was veiled, frantic thoughts consuming her and momentarily pulling her in opposing directions. What on earth was she doing? How could she have let things go so far? But she knew why. Her mind was as clear as a pane of glass on the fact that she wanted him. After all, she had wanted him for what felt like half a lifetime even though she knew it was senseless. She doubted that any other man would ever make her feel as he did. So why should she not finally go to bed with her own husband? Why should she not find out what sex was like before they divorced? She could live out a little harmless fantasy, a little voice whispered seductively in the back of her mind. It would be a risk-free venture that would cost her nothing but a little pride.

'Prudence…' Nik murmured huskily, saying it like a guy getting into practice, his Greek accent scissoring carefully round the syllables. 'Don't look so worried, *pethi mou*. There isn't a problem in the world I can't sort.'

He leant over her and drove her lips apart in an explosive kiss. It was as if a ball of energy had ignited inside her. Her heart thumped like crazy and she quivered as the sweet flood-tide of desire flared, making her achingly aware of every inch of her body. When he shaped her breasts she arched her spine to press the excruciatingly tender, rosy peaks into his palms. He laved the tortured tips with his tongue and she moaned with impassioned abandon while he proceeded with all the skill in his repertoire to dispose of her remaining garments without her noticing.

When he traced the delicate softness below the nest of curls at the apex of her thighs she trembled, mortified by the moist heat at the heart of her receptive body. The fierce surge of excitement that followed shattered her expectations. Suddenly, thought was no longer possible and she was writhing, her hips shifting on the bed as he tantalised the most sensitive spot of all with expert fingers and explored the slick wet heat of her.

'Will I be the first?' Nik husked, coiling back from her to strip off his trousers.

With difficulty she focused on him and she was shaken by her desire to tell him that no, he would not be, even if it would be the most awful lie.

As the silence lengthened, tension screamed through Nik's big, powerful frame: had she been with someone else?

Her gaze locked to his lean darkly handsome face and her heartbeat raced. She discovered she could not lie to him on that score. 'Yes...'

Raw relief drenched Nik in a rush of gratitude to the fates. Clad only in his shorts, he came back to her to curve long brown fingers to her cheekbone with an almost clumsy tenderness that was unfamiliar to her. 'I had no right to expect or even to hope...but that you are a virgin will mean a great deal to me,' he swore, speaking half in English, half in Greek.

'Will it?' She shut her eyes tight because they were prickling with tears.

'Of course...you are my bride and you will know no other man,' Nik rasped half under his breath.

As he eased back from her to finish undressing, Prudence did not let her attention stray from him for a second. Her breathing grew quick and shallow. From the steely contours of his shoulders to his long, powerful, hair-roughened thighs he looked spectacular. He had the broad, muscular chest, the sleek, iron-hard torso and the lean hips of a natural athlete. He removed his shorts and she almost stopped breathing altogether. She was shocked by her first glimpse of a fully grown male in a state of rampant arousal.

'If I had waited another few minutes I wouldn't have needed to ask whether or not you were a virgin,' Nik murmured with unholy amusement lighting his eyes to pure golden enticement. 'Your face says it all.'

Dropping down on the bed beside her, he ravished her reddened mouth with passionate thoroughness. A wave of heat consumed her. The tender flesh between her legs was shamefully moist. With a husky sound of male appreciation he let his teeth graze the achingly stiff bud of a swollen pink nipple and slowly and surely he rediscovered the slick dampness that betrayed her need. Her lips parted on a long-drawn-out moan and she clenched her teeth on a pleasure that came close to pain. Her excitement built up in layer on layer until she could hardly get air into her lungs.

'I didn't know I could feel like this…'

His scorching gaze welded to hers. 'Not everyone can. Your passion matches mine.'

She drowned in the hot, sweet pleasure of his caresses. She could not stay still. Beyond all thought, she surrendered to sensation until it seemed that the torment of such craving would tear her in two. 'Please…' she gasped then.

Nik arranged her under him, sliding fluidly between her thighs. 'I may hurt you,' he warned her unevenly, his lithe, bronzed length ferociously tense over hers.

'S'OK,' she mumbled, dry-mouthed, her entire body thrumming with the intolerable hunger.

'I want it to be perfect…' he swore raggedly, stunning golden eyes locked to hers with passionate resolve.

He tipped her back and eased degree by degree into her slick, tight depths. Her eyes widened at the fullness of him. He breached the barrier that would have repelled him with a single thrust. The stab of pain was an unwelcome surprise. 'Oh, my goodness…Nik—'

'Shush…it'll get better. I promise,' he husked raggedly, sinking his hands beneath her to cup her hips and steadily deepen his penetration.

'Don't move…' she begged, waiting for the discomfort to recede.

'I hurt you,' Nik groaned, rigid with the tension of exerting such fierce control over his overeager body. 'But you're very small.'

Prudence allowed herself a minor exploratory wriggle and then another. A cat-that-got-the-cream expression crept over her absorbed face as sensation returned in abundance. He felt incredible inside her. The erotic pulse of desire controlled her again and she angled up to him in encouragement until he lifted her to meet his primal thrust. Her heart started to pound, her voice to catch in her throat. His every fluid movement engulfed her in sensual pleasure. He moved in slow provocation at first and then skilfully increased his rhythm. Wild excitement seized her. When she reached a fever pitch of unbearable sensation, he took her higher still into a shattering crescendo of ecstasy. Crying out his name in a frenzy of delight, she lost herself entirely in the blissful aftershocks of sweet pleasure.

In a daze, Nik rolled back against the pillows and held her close. He was trembling, in shock after the longest, hottest release of his life. She shifted in his arms and he tightened his grip on her. Well, she wasn't going any place now…except home with him. Home where? The apartment really wasn't suitable. It was a playboy's pad, not the place for Prudence. They could live in a hotel for a while. He would have to buy a house. What about all the animals? A house in the country within easy reach of London. He pressed a kiss like a benediction to her smooth brow. 'That was awesome, *pethi mou*.'

Prudence breathed in the hot, damp, wonderfully familiar scent of his skin. Her head was still swimming, her body languorous from the glorious surfeit of pleasure. In quiet, appreciative silence she revelled in a rare moment of pure, unvarnished happiness. Try as she might, though, she could not shut out her thoughts and just as fast the clouds rolled in. In going to bed with Nik she had been living out a fantasy, she reminded herself. In time-honoured style, he had been fantastic and he had fully justified his wild reputation, she reflected with a pain she refused to acknowledge. But wasn't it a bit sad of her to be still clinging and pretending he was a real, loving, caring husband *after* the main event was over? Wasn't it time for her to get back to the real world?

Nik let long brown fingers slide through the tumbling mass of chestnut hair spilling across his chest. 'You're very quiet.'

A sparkling smile fixed like glue to her reddened lips, Prudence lifted her tousled head. 'I was just thinking how good you are at all this stuff…now I finally know what all the fuss is about—'

Dazzling golden eyes zeroed in on her, bright as hot sunlight in his lean, darkly handsome face. He frowned, wondering if she was trying to make him laugh to cover her awkwardness. 'I'm not quite sure those are the sentiments I want to hear from my wife…'

Anger tensed Prudence, for that label always hit her like a cruel taunt, a reminder of what their relationship had not been. She had never felt married and sleeping with Nik didn't change that. Suddenly she was feeling very much like a woman who had made a major mistake. In a sudden movement she scrambled free of him.

'What is the matter with you?' Nik demanded, hoisting himself up against the tumbled pillows, bronzed skin startlingly dark against the delicate white and pink bedlinen.

Snatching up her wrap, Prudence dug her arms into it, desperate to cover up her voluptuous curves. 'Sharing a bed with me doesn't make me your wife. It just makes me one more in a long line of women!' she heard herself toss in furious rebuttal. 'And you're not exactly exclusive, are you?'

Nik was poleaxed by that response. He vaulted out of bed but she had already stalked out of the room. In the act of following her, he registered that it was still daylight and that there were no curtains drawn. Quietly cursing up a storm, he began to hurriedly pull on his clothes again.

Her face tight with suppressed emotion, Prudence sidled

back into the doorway. 'I'm sorry I was rude like that. There's never any excuse for bad manners,' she said stiffly, refusing to meet his lancing dark golden gaze. 'But I do still want a divorce—'

Nik was insulted beyond belief by that announcement. 'Why the hell did you let me take you to bed?'

Prudence almost cringed. 'I'd really rather not discuss that—'

'No flannel…you owe me the truth!' Nik raked back at her rawly.

Wild horses could not have forced Prudence to look at him. Her cheeks scarlet, she compressed her ripe mouth and breathed in very deep. 'I just wanted to know what it would be like with you. I didn't think it would be any big deal on your terms.'

In such a rage that he could hardly vocalise, Nik studied her. There she was, all five feet two of her and she was confessing to using him like some stud on trial. 'I don't believe you. I don't believe you still want a divorce either. You still care about me. I think that's why you gave me your virginity.'

That bold, challenging statement sliced like a sharp knife through every layer of her tender skin. That Nik should confront her with her feelings for him was her worst nightmare come true and she knew she would never forgive him for it. Pride brought up her head, blue eyes defiant and bright. 'Maybe I was just tired of being a virgin. I don't still care about you in that way, Nik,' she asserted. 'I was infatuated with you when we married but it didn't last the course. I got over you a very long time ago.'

'Those scrapbooks sing a different song,' Nik delivered with a cruel edge he had never used around her before.

Shock at that immediate, unhesitating retaliation made Prudence turn white as snow, nausea stirring in her stomach. 'I want you to leave. You're not welcome here any more!' she told him jerkily. 'I'm going for a divorce and I don't need your permission for it!'

'I forgot to give you your birthday present.' Nik extended a slim jewellery case as if she hadn't spoken.

Prudence sucked in a sustaining breath. Curiosity warred with the need to keep him at a distance. Curiosity won. She stared down at the incredibly pretty diamond-studded pendant in the shape of a…? He had the neck to give her a heart when he had smashed her own into a thousand pieces? Eyes burning with boiling tears, she snapped the case shut again and forced it back into his hand. 'Thanks, but I don't want it or you… Now go away!'

Slamming the door shut on his exit, she leant back against it and listened to the helicopter taking off again. Anger and pain and despair coalesced inside her. She would probably never see him again. She had insulted him. Everything she had valued about their relationship had been destroyed by a reckless bout of sex. The trust, the respect, the affection were gone. How could she even blame Nik for coming on to her? In her opinion he knew no other way to relate to a woman. But what madness had possessed her? The dull, intimate ache between her thighs made her shamed face burn. The besotted teenager whom she believed she had outgrown had had her swansong after all. But the aftermath of regret was hurting her much more than she could have believed.

It was, she sensed painfully, the end of an era. Eight years ago she had flown out to Greece and her life had been driven off course. Taking back the initiative meant moving on from that past. Swallowing back the dark thickness of tears clogging her throat, she reminded herself why she wanted her freedom back. In a couple of years she might have a child of her own to love and care for but she had to start divorce proceedings first and inform her grandfather of her intentions…

CHAPTER THREE

PRUDENCE UNFURLED THE letter from her solicitor, Mr Bullen, and her expressive eyes widened as she read. 'I don't believe it!'

'What don't you believe?' A mug of tea clasped in one hand, Leo paused in the act of shunting Prudence's two slumbering dogs off the kitchen sofa.

'Nik!' Prudence, renowned for her lack of temper and easy, tolerant nature, was pacing the cluttered kitchen in a fever of emotion. 'My solicitor hasn't even drawn up my divorce petition yet, but Nik's fancy legal team have already been in touch with him.'

'To say what?' Leo prompted.

'That Nik has no intention of giving his consent to a divorce... How can he even consider doing that to me? Without his consent, I'll have to wait five years to get my freedom!'

'He told you he didn't want a divorce,' the blond man reminded her wryly.

Prudence stared fixedly at the old jug on the table. It was stuffed to over-capacity with gorgeous pink and white roses. In fact, there was not a room in the house that was not full of glorious blooms, for Nik had sent her flowers every day of the two weeks that had passed since her birthday. No doubt his PA had organised the extravagant floral schedule, she thought waspishly. On a more personal level, however, Nik had phoned and she had left him talking to the answering machine until frustration drove him into flying down to see her again. The instant she had heard the helicopter hovering overhead she had jumped into her car and driven off. After all, what did she have left to say to him? she had asked herself. Or he to her? Only now was she recognising the flaw in her reasoning and the innate stupidity of practising avoidance tactics on a male as confrontational as Nik.

But Prudence still had no idea why he was behaving as he was. Why was he blocking her desire for a divorce? They had lived separate lives almost from the day of their marriage. She had dismissed the objections he had voiced a fortnight earlier: she had assumed that he was just going through the motions, acting out a conventional concern when he didn't really care either way. Now she was being forced to accept that Nik meant business. She had gone to bed with him as well. Heated memories of that event made her anxious face colour. Had her weakness, her very willingness hardened his attitude? Had she, in fact, acted as her own worst enemy?

'Are you still going up to London to attend that lecture later?' she asked Leo.

He nodded. 'Why?'

'If Nik's free, I might ask you to give me a lift.'

In her bedroom, she dialled Nik direct. 'Nik? It's Prudence…'

Nik dismissed the staff surrounding him with a peremptory gesture. A brooding smile forming on his lean, dark face, for he had been expecting her call, he lounged back against his polished granite desk in an attitude of relaxation that would have infuriated her had she seen it. 'How are you?'

'Not very good actually,' Prudence confided truthfully. 'I'll be in London this afternoon. Could we talk then?'

'Four o'clock, at my apartment,' Nik suggested in a tone of the utmost pleasantness. 'I look forward to seeing you.'

Prudence had had a couple of weeks to calm down and think matters over, Nik reflected. She now knew that there was no question of her gaining a divorce in the short term. So why would she still want to throw away the terrific understanding that they had always shared? Surely she would be more ready to appreciate that he could be a great husband if he chose to be? And that if she had wanted that demonstration eight years ago, she should have behaved like a wife and stayed with him, not run as fast and as far as she could go!

Nik had found it an ordeal to play a waiting game with Prudence for two long weeks. When he met opposition, he liked to act fast and hit back hard. He did not want a divorce. He had said so and she hadn't listened. But he was reining back his natural aggression in an effort to gently and patiently persuade Prudence round to his viewpoint. He could not credit that she would withstand such a campaign.

He was even willing to concede that he had a credibility problem in the matrimonial stakes. His own lawyers had barely managed to conceal their astonishment when he informed them that he would fight the divorce that his wife was planning every step of the way. And when Theo Demakis had visited to commiserate with him about Prudence's "stupidity", Nik had been so disgusted by the abusive way in which the older man spoke of his granddaughter that he had finally told Theo exactly what he thought of him. As a result of that outbreak of frank speech, Nik fully expected to find himself involved in a bitter trade war with Demakis International, for Theo was not the man to take his come-uppance lying down.

When Prudence climbed into Leo's comfortable car at noon, he was chatting on his mobile phone. She was a patient audi-

ence while Leo talked his late friend's widow, Stella, through
what to do with a leaking radiator. It was two years since Leo's
best friend had died of cancer, leaving Stella with three young
children. Leo was a regular visitor at her home. Whether he
would ever work up the courage to tell Stella that he was
madly in love with her was not something Prudence had ever
dared to ask, since Leo's guilty secret was that he had fallen
for his friend's wife long before she became a widow.

'I was going to call round later…oh, right,' Leo was saying in a tone of forced joviality. 'No, of course I don't disapprove! I think it's great that you're going out and about again.'

Leo set aside the phone and ignited the engine. 'Stella's
going out for a drink with friends.'

'I heard.'

'This is just the beginning…she's a very attractive woman,'
he breathed morosely. 'She'll have a boyfriend in no time.'

Prudence said nothing. Leo was in a horrible situation. He
could speak up and risk destroying his current relationship
with Stella, who might well be horrified by the feelings he revealed. Or he could stay silent and suffer while some other
man filled the empty space in her life. There was no easy answer. In the act of giving his arm a sympathetic squeeze,
Prudence frowned at the sight of the two men erecting a 'For
Sale' board at the foot of the farm lane.

'What on earth are they doing?' Leo exclaimed.

Prudence got out of the car and tackled the workmen.
When she told them that they were putting the sign up at the
wrong property she was shown a worksheet that listed her
home, Craighill Farm. She used her mobile phone to ring
their boss, who suggested she take the matter up with the estate agent.

Leo drove on while Prudence tried to get hold of the agent.
He was unavailable. A salesman informed her that Craighill

Farm was to be surveyed for the sales brochure the following day. Having pointed out that she lived there and knew nothing about any such arrangement, she requested the name of the supposed vendor and was informed that that was confidential information. Coming off the phone again in exasperation, she sighed. 'I'll sort it out with the agent later. Why is it that nobody will ever accept responsibility for a silly mistake?'

Nik lived in a vast London apartment complete with a roof garden and a pool. Prudence had been there lots of times but had never felt at home with its sleek designer furniture, the modern sculptures or wide, echoing swathes of marble floor. Her nerves were on edge long before she even emerged from the lift. Having resisted all urges to dress up until she lost her nerve at the eleventh hour, she was wearing a long brown skirt and a cream gypsy top that was a little too tight for her to relax in. But she *would* relax, she assured herself staunchly. As long as she suppressed all memory of that unfortunate episode in the bedroom and kept her temper, there was every chance that she could recapture her former easy-going relationship with Nik.

'Prudence…' All cool and sophistication in a light grey business suit, Nik crossed the imposing lounge to greet her. He looked shockingly handsome: lean, mean and darkly magnificent.

Attacked from within by a flashing recollection of him stripping by the side of her bed, Prudence turned scarlet and froze to the spot.

Nik closed a lean hand over hers and walked her back across the room with breathtaking assurance. 'You look sexy in that top—'

'Don't say stuff like that!' Prudence told him in consternation.

Nik came to a slow halt and gazed down at her, the dense black fringe of his lashes accentuating the flaring gold of his eyes. 'Everything's different. You can't pretend it didn't happen—'

'Yes we can if we want to!'

His golden eyes smouldered. 'But I don't want to forget the longest, hottest climax I've ever had,' he spelt out succinctly. 'In fact, I would much prefer to—'

Aghast at his candour, Prudence planted a harried forefinger in a silencing gesture against his full lower lip. *'Please…'*

Nik ran the tip of his tongue down her finger into the palm of her hand while she stood there transfixed and trembling. Her breasts rose and fell with the rapid, shallow breaths she was taking and she was unbearably conscious of the tingling tightening of her nipples inside her bra. She could not credit what he was doing to her. She was both appalled and fascinated. He curled her fingers into his, lifted his arrogant dark head and breathed huskily, 'So I want to go to bed and you want to talk—'

In a heroic effort to fight her own helpless craving, Prudence stepped away from him. 'I'm only here because you told your lawyers you won't consent to a divorce.'

'So which part of that did you misunderstand?' Nik enquired with insolent assurance. 'I have no intention of changing my mind.'

'But why?' Prudence demanded helplessly. 'I can't understand why.'

'When I married you, I married you for life. You're my wife. I will not willingly let you divorce me. Of course, I will have no choice in five years—'

'But you can't ask me to put my life on hold for five years!'

A slow-burning smile curved Nik's lean, strong face. 'I'm not. I believe I'm an improvement on a sperm bank…'

Angered by that crack, she threw back her head, glossy brown hair tumbling back from her flushed face. 'You may like to think so—'

'I *know* so. Of course, it's a moot point if there's another man involved in your wish for a divorce,' Nik purred very softly, his entire attention welded to her.

'Is that what this is all about? You think that you might be in some sort of macho competition? Why can't you accept that I simply do not want to be married to you any longer?' Prudence slung at him with fierce sincerity.

'But you've never been married to me in the normal sense of the word,' Nik contended in a tone of cold implacability that was new to her.

Prudence could feel emotion swelling inside her like a dangerous riptide. Keeping her back straight, she walked over to the window, striving with all her might to appear controlled and composed. 'And I don't *want* to be. We were friends. I liked that. But that's it; that's as much as I can handle!'

Tears were prickling the backs of her eyes but she had complete faith in what she was telling him. Nik needed a wife who would be content with a superficial show of marital togetherness and turn a blind eye to his mistresses. A wife who would accept money and status in place of his heart or his attention. Prudence knew that she was not capable of taking on that role. He was a bred-in-the-bone womaniser with a taste for gorgeous supermodels whom no average woman could ever hope to rival. He would be unfaithful and she would not be able to bear it. It would destroy her…*he* would destroy her if she was not strong enough to resist him. That was why she would not allow herself to be tempted by the illusion of the real marriage that he was offering her.

'You slept with me. That changed the rules of the game,' Nik delivered with razor-edged cool.

An odd little shiver ran down her spine. She stole a glance at him, clashed with scorching golden eyes and felt a tiny twist of heat low in her pelvis. 'It's not a game—'

'The way you're behaving makes it feel like one. Have you any idea yet whether or not you're pregnant?' Nik asked levelly. 'Or is it too soon to tell?'

That casual question threw Prudence into a startled loop. 'Pregnant?' she parroted in shock. 'You mean you didn't—?'

'When you let me take you to bed, I naturally assumed that an ongoing marriage was a done deal.' Nik studied her with steady golden eyes and she squirmed and lowered her lashes in guilty self-defence. 'You told me how much you wanted a baby, so I saw no point in using contraception.'

'You should have said—'

'It was for you to notice. If you didn't notice, I must have been good.' Nik sent her a sizzling look of amusement that was as physical as a caress and sent her heart racing. 'It was the first time I've ever made love without a contraceptive... I have to confess that I liked it. I liked it a hell of a lot.'

Already reeling with shock at his revelation, Prudence was burning up with mortification. With difficulty she thought over what he had confessed. Evading his gaze, she muttered stiltedly, 'It's not that easy to get pregnant, you know—'

'No, I don't. I'm happy to admit ignorance on that score—'

'I should think it's extremely unlikely that it would happen.' Prudence was outraged by his earthy attitude and the humour he had shown.

'Give me a month. I'm a goal-orientated guy—'

Hot, bothered and infuriated by that comeback, Prudence seized on a more positive statement to silence him. 'I'm absolutely certain that I'm not pregnant,' she told him, believing that she was not really lying and that within a couple of days her body would give her the proof that she was right in her conviction.

'That's unfortunate. But then for the moment I can only hope that common sense persuades you that rushing into the role of an unmarried mother is a very bad idea,' Nik said drily.

'I have a comfortable home and the trust fund my aunt put in my name for Mum and me—'

'That fund is so tiny it doesn't count—'

'But I don't have champagne tastes. I'll work as well. Either way, I'll have enough to raise a child,' Prudence contended.

'Material considerations are only one side of the equation. I have other objections. Every child deserves a father—'

'I got by without one—'

'Some might say his absence left you with a distinctly low opinion of men,' Nik shot at her, his dark golden eyes grim. 'Even if I wasn't your husband I would have serious reservations about your plans. Raising children is challenging enough for two parents, never mind one. What if you were to fall ill? What if the child is born with a disability?'

Prudence was very pale. 'I've thought of those things… I'll manage. I've really thought this through. I believe I have enough to offer.'

Nik released his breath in an impatient hiss. 'You're more like your grandfather than I ever appreciated. When Theo Demakis wants something, he suffers from the same stubborn tunnel vision.'

Sincerely hurt and offended by that comparison, Prudence gave him a furious look. 'I'm not stubborn… I'm not at all like him!'

'At least learn by Theo's mistakes within his own family circle. A child should have the chance to enjoy the benefits of a family life with a father and a conventional home environment.'

Wounded by his apparent conviction that she could not offer a child a tithe of what that little girl or boy deserved and needed, Prudence tilted her chin. 'Such as you would offer? Have you the nerve to suggest that you could offer any woman a normal family life?'

'Yes, I have that nerve.'

Three mistresses in three different countries, Prudence reflected in a passion of painful resentment. Normal? Conventional? How dared he criticise her quiet and decent country lifestyle and suggest that he could do better?

'It's amazing that you should want to stay married to me after all this time,' Prudence contended angrily. 'Why are you so reluctant to divorce me? Do you know what I'm beginning to think? I'm *still* Theo Demakis's granddaughter—'

His lean, intelligent face set taut with tension while his stunning dark eyes took on a forbidding aspect. 'Don't say it,' he breathed. 'Don't go down that road to insult me.'

Prudence was too upset to heed that warning. Her every instinct was urging her to fight back. 'Perhaps you still believe I could be a financial asset to you. My grandfather may not be speaking to me right now but—'

'I threw Theo out of my office last week. He was in a rage about your divorce plans. He seemed to think you had phoned him to tell him that news out of pure malice and he informed me that he had cut you out of his will.'

'You threw him out…oh,' Prudence mumbled uncomfortably, unable to meet his gaze, for she was ashamed of herself for throwing the slur that would draw the most blood. She knew it had no basis in fact. Nik was very proud and his sense of honour strong. He would never have married her to save his own financial skin but he had found it impossible to stand by and watch his family suffer the ignominy of bankruptcy. As for that news about her grandfather's will, she spared it barely a thought because she had never dreamt that anyone who disliked her so thoroughly would consider leaving her anything.

'So, you don't figure as a profitable enterprise in any way. In fact, staying married to you might even be bad for business because Theo is a very bitter man right now,' Nik imparted between clenched teeth of restraint. 'As you're also aware, it's several years since I paid back your dowry with interest. I owe Theo nothing and, when he's as rude as he was about you last week, not even the time of day.'

Prudence winced at the revelation that defending her name had pitched him into a battle with the older man. 'I know…I accept that. I shouldn't have said that about the money—'

'But you did say it and I won't forget it,' Nik swore darkly. 'I'm well aware that my family profited from our marriage in a way that you and your mother did not. But you have stone-walled my every attempt to redress that balance. You have always refused to accept an allowance from me—'

'Oh, Nik, please, don't say any more,' Prudence urged in a stifled voice of distress and regret that she had reduced their relationship to such a mercenary level that he felt he had to defend his own behaviour. 'We didn't have a proper marriage, so I couldn't possibly have accepted money from you. It just wouldn't have felt right. You helped out in lots of other ways. When Mum was ill, with the nursing expenses, and other things—when I needed shelters for the animals and extra food…'

'I am only asking you to give our marriage a chance,' Nik ground out in a driven undertone. 'What would that cost you?'

Prudence let her strained blue eyes linger on his lean, bronzed features for a split-second and hurriedly looked away again. But even that one stolen appraisal dazzled her, just as he had dazzled her the very first time she saw him eight years ago. If he had had the slightest idea what it would cost her he would not have asked that question. Once she had been obsessed with him. Was that the Demakis blood in her veins? Was that why she had found it so very hard to let go of loving Nik? But, having mastered that love and distilled all that energy into friendship and acceptance that she could never have anything more, she was terrified of exposing herself to that much pain again.

'I can't…I just can't,' she said flatly and, glancing down with relief at her watch, she began walking hurriedly to the door. 'I must go—'

'You've only been here half an hour—'

'I have to meet Leo at six and you and I have already said all there is to say. I don't want to say the things I'm saying to you…it's upsetting me,' she condemned chokily.

Incensed at the very mention of the other man's name, Nik caught her hand to pull her back before she could make it out through the front door. 'And doesn't that tell you something?' he growled in a driven undertone. 'If you fight me you will get hurt, and that isn't what I want either.'

'I can't believe that you know *what* you want—'

'Don't I? Am I so bad at putting my message across?' A dangerous light in his shimmering dark golden eyes, Nik brought his sensual mouth crashing down on hers.

Astonishment gripped her, for there was nothing cool or sophisticated about caveman tactics. But she found that scorching onslaught as shockingly exciting as the domineering way he hauled her up against him. She kissed him back with bittersweet fervour, opening her mouth for the ravishing quest of his tongue. Her heart was pounding into a crazy crescendo. Her body felt tight and hot and oversensitive. She was pushing closer, burrowing in the hard-muscled contours of his powerful frame. And then her subconscious mind served up an image that cut right through that passion. Her memory leapfrogged back to her wedding day and the moment that she had seen Nik kissing Cassia Morikis. That was when she had truly understood that even a wedding ring could not bind Nikolos Angelis to her and make him hers in the way she needed him to be.

Yanking herself free of him, she rubbed a hand across her reddened lips as if to deny the taste of him. 'You shouldn't have done that!'

Prudence tottered into the lift on wobbling legs and let it carry her down to the ground floor. She felt emotionally battered, but her body was still alight with the passion Nik had awakened and the ache of desire made her despise herself even more. It was the stuff of nightmares for her to emerge from the building and find that she was the target of cameras and shouted questions from a crowd of journalists wielding microphones. For a split-second she was paralysed, as blind and helpless as a rabbit caught in car headlights.

'Is it true you're divorcing Nik, Mrs Angelis?'

'Does Nik want to marry someone else?'

'Any truth in the rumour that your grandfather begged him to stay married to you?'

CHAPTER FOUR

'DON'T BE STUPID!' Prudence heard herself say before she got wise and simply turned on her heels and ran for her life.

She did not stop until she had outrun the pack of journalists following her down the street. Gulping in fresh air, she took a careful look around her and slowed her pace; the paparazzi had gone. It had been an enervating episode for a woman who was not accustomed to media interest. Her face had only made it into the newspapers twice since her marriage—and only then at private events held to bring in funds for the sanctuary. It shook her to acknowledge that Nik lived with that kind of attention every day.

For the first time she allowed herself to mull over the astonishing fact that Nik had been willing to run the risk of getting her pregnant to keep her. At heart Nik could be very basic. Naïve as well, she thought ruefully. According to what she had read, it was quite common for couples to have to spend a year trying for a baby. The same gloomy book had informed her that even though she was only in her late twenties, her most fertile years already lay behind her. On that basis she thought there was virtually no chance that conception could have taken place on the strength of a single occasion.

When she met up with Leo again, he looked as grim as she felt.

'What's up?' she asked.

'I ran into a friend of Stella's at the lecture. She let drop that Stella's actually going out on a date tonight with some guy…she just didn't know how to tell me and thought I would disapprove.'

Prudence winced and tucked her hand into the crook of his elbow. 'Oh, dear. Mind you, she has been on her own for two years now.'

'I know that.' Leo settled frustrated brown eyes on her. 'Give me the female viewpoint. Advise me on my next move…'

'I can't…I can't! *You* have to make that decision.'

'I've got too much to lose,' Leo sighed. 'Look, let's have dinner before we drive back. It's not like I've got anything better to do.'

'How did you get on with Nik this afternoon?' he finally enquired while they were studying their menus in the restaurant.

Prudence tried to hoist her usual bright smile onto her mouth and failed. She thought of the fact that her relationship with Nik now lay in broken pieces. She thought of the fact that he was cruelly forcing her to continually reject the marriage that had once been her naïve and foolish dream. And to her horror and without the slightest warning, tears sprouted into her eyes and poured in a flood down her cheeks.

'Prudence…' Leo was horrified and palpably embarrassed and he gripped the hand she had rested on the table. 'Shall we leave?'

'No, I'll be all right in a minute…sorry,' she told him ruefully, fumbling for a tissue and smiling apologetically at him through her tears.

Somewhere very close a camera flashed. Leo blinked and released his hold on her to shoot upright. 'That bloke just took a photo of us! What's going on?'

'I must have been followed from Nik's apartment. I thought I'd shaken the reporters off, but obviously I was wrong,' Prudence sighed, mopping her face dry.

Leo stayed upright, making it clear that he would still prefer to leave. 'You should have warned me…I had no idea you attracted this kind of attention when you were in London.'

'I don't as a rule, but word seems to have leaked out about the divorce and evidently anything to do with Nik's private life is news. The paparazzi adore him.' It crossed Prudence's mind that, put in the same position as Leo, Nik would have shrugged and stayed to eat. But then Nik had a magnificent disregard for incidents that embarrassed other people. She felt guilty for comparing him to Leo, who was more sensitive and not at all arrogant.

On the drive back home, Leo told her that he had applied for a teaching position in London. A pang of dismay assailed her, for if he was successful he would be selling up and moving to the city and she would miss his company. Yet she also appreciated that such a move would make sense for him now that his father was no longer alive.

Only when Leo had finished telling Prudence about his plans was she free to ponder her own predicament. It seemed to her that she was in a no-win situation. If she continued with the divorce proceedings in the teeth of Nik's opposition she would be wasting money she didn't have on legal bills. She would have to find another way of changing Nik's mind. Of course, a really bold woman would not allow Nik to come between her and her future plans, Prudence reflected ruefully. A really bold woman would head off to the sperm bank regardless, reflecting that she had *asked* for a divorce and that if her subsequent fertility caused her husband embarrassment and some denials, it would be entirely his own fault. But even though she was angry with both Nik and her grandfather, she did not wish to affront either man to that extent.

A strange car was parked in the yard at her home. Annoyed that the 'For Sale' board was still there at the foot of the lane, Prudence was hoping that the car belonged to the estate agent so that she could give him a piece of her mind. A small, pugnacious man in a suit got out of the car and approached her. 'Mrs Prudence Angelis…?'

Prudence nodded confirmation. 'Yes?'

He handed her a document and got straight back into his car to drive off again. She opened it up. It was an eviction notice drawn up by her grandfather's legal firm in London.

Her solicitor, Mr Bullen, was able to see her first thing the next morning. He studied the notice she had been served with and sighed. 'Yes, I'm afraid it's in order. Your mother was warned that this could happen some day.'

'My mother, Trixie…*knew* that there was a risk of this? She never mentioned it to me. I don't understand,' Prudence protested, her eyes shadowed by the horrible sleepless night of worry she had endured.

'As you know, my colleague, who handled your late mother's estate, retired last year. He may well have assumed that your mother had already explained the intricacies of your position and that you understood the problems.'

'I thought I did, but I obviously didn't. I knew that I would never *own* Craighill Farm. But I believed that it was mine to use for my lifetime.'

'The farm belongs to your grandfather and he has always had the right to ask you to vacate the property so that it can be sold. The agreement by which your mother acquired the right to live at Craighill was extremely complex. In it, however, your grandfather, Theo Demakis, clearly reserved the right to put an end to the agreement at any time and he has now chosen to exercise that option.' The solicitor surveyed his client with a curiosity he could not conceal. 'Of course you could purchase Craighill Farm for your own use and that would soon settle the problem.'

Prudence stretched her mouth into as good a semblance of an unconcerned smile as she could manage. She was fully conscious that while she carried the name Angelis a plea of poverty was unlikely to receive a sympathetic hearing. She walked slowly back out to her battered four-wheel-drive. She felt traumatised. She was to move out of the farm within the month. It was a bad moment to appreciate that, whenever trouble loomed on her horizon, she was accustomed to phoning Nik. He had always been her first port of call in a tight corner and his advice and guidance had proved invaluable a dozen times in the past. But she couldn't phone Nik for support this time, could she?

There was certainly no point contacting her Greek grandfather, who had made his animosity clear with a speed and a ferocity that appalled her. Evidently, her decision to divorce Nik had been the last straw. In her ignorance she had believed that her father, Apollo, had funded the purchase of the farm and that it would be her home until the end of her days. The truth had come as a severe shock. Why should her grandfather let her continue to live in his property when as far as he was concerned she was a rubbish granddaughter? Theo Demakis owed her nothing, she conceded wretchedly.

In less than a month, every animal in the sanctuary would be homeless. It was as if a bomb had exploded under her tidy little world. With it went all her dreams. To think she had believed that she was financially secure enough to contemplate

single-parenthood! Only now did she see that her freedom
from having to pay either rent or a mortgage had been the
foundation of her security and that without that advantage all
her plans came apart at the seams.

But she was being horribly selfish when all she could think
about were her own problems, she acknowledged guiltily.
Dottie and Sam Trent lived at Craighill as well. Where would
they move to? She had let the cottage to them and cheerfully
assured them that they could live there for as long as they
liked. She felt sick at that recollection.

Skilled at handling difficult patients, Dottie had come to
nurse Trixie at a time when Prudence was struggling to cope.
Within weeks, Dottie and her husband had become keen vol-
unteers at the sanctuary. But soon after Trixie's death, Sam
had had a stroke and Dottie had been unable to work. The
kindly couple had got into financial difficulty through no
fault of their own and that was when Prudence had extended
a helping hand. Her generosity had been repaid a hundred
times over and Sam's health had improved steadily but the
older man would never recover full mobility. The Trents
would be utterly devastated if they lost their home for a second time.

Prudence got back to the farm just in time for the estate
agent's visit. When he told her what he believed the property
would fetch on the open market, she was appalled: it was an
amount as far out of her reach as the stars. Even so, she made
an appointment with her bank for the following day so that
she could find out if there was any way she could borrow the
money. She was informed that she had no assets to offer as
security and that she did not earn enough to meet the payments. The loan officer at the building society she approached
was equally deflating.

Her heart sank and her pride cringed as it slowly and painfully dawned on her that the only person she could turn to for help was Nik. Before she could lose her nerve, she rang him.

'I need to see you… urgently!' she confided in a rush.

His lean, strong face etched in forbidding lines, Nik surveyed the newspaper spread out on his desk and the grainy photo of his wife holding hands with her very good friend, Leo. 'In relation to what?'

Prudence worried at her lower lip. 'I've had a bit of a shock. I'm in a serious fix. Would you consider giving me a loan? You'd probably have to stretch the payments over about a hundred years,' she warned him apprehensively.

'Explain…' Interest had sparked like a hot flame in his brooding dark gaze.

'If I can't buy Craighill, the sanctuary will have to close and I don't know where the animals will go… You see, I don't have the right to live there that I thought I had. Grandfather is selling the farm over my head,' she told him unevenly.

Nik sprang upright and his smile was colder than ice. *Thank you, Theo.* Homeless animals—just what he needed as a lever; he was back on track again. He absorbed the remainder of her explanation without interruption. 'OK. I can fly down tomorrow morning but it'll be very early.'

Nik's helicopter landed at seven.

Her heart thumping fast behind her breastbone, Prudence watched him stride towards her. Two sleepless nights in succession had lowered her resistance level to his sensational dark good looks. Lean, bronzed features serious, he didn't smile, however, and that spooked her. Even had she not been painfully aware of just how much was riding on his response to her request, his demeanour would have warned her that success was by no means a foregone conclusion. A little *frisson* of apprehension slivered through her tense frame.

'Would you like coffee?'

'No, thanks. I can only stay half an hour. I have to be in Athens by early afternoon,' Nik drawled smoothly, looking at the way her pink top defined the luscious swell of her breasts, remembering, then hastily shutting down on that imagery as his body reacted with extraordinary enthusiasm. He didn't look back at her until he felt colder than ice.

'Right…well…you might as well see this…' Prudence handed the eviction notice to him and started talking very fast about what the solicitor had told her the day before.

'You explained the situation yesterday.'

'I don't understand how my own grandfather can do this to me,' she confessed unhappily.

'Theo's a bad loser…as I fall into the same category, it would be unwise for me to pass comment.'

Prudence collided unwarily with a look from Nik that was as dark and cool as the sky at midnight. 'But you wouldn't be callous and cruel like that!'

'Let's treat this as a business transaction,' Nik suggested.

Prudence went pink and accepted the return of the papers she had pressed on him. 'The bank won't give me a loan.'

'Of course they won't. The very fact that you had to approach them, rather than me, would look bad.'

Prudence heaved a sigh. 'Yes, I did get that message. My solicitor seemed to assume I would just be able to buy the farm—'

'Which, of course, you would have been able to do…had you ever accepted the allowance I tried to give you—'

'But I don't want you to *give* me money,' Prudence pointed out hastily. 'That would be wrong. I want to borrow it from you—'

'You said that the property is on the market for seven hundred thousand pounds. Nobody in their right mind would sad-

dle you with a debt you have no current prospect of re-
paying—'

'If you gave me a long enough time—'

'No,' Nik incised without hesitation. 'I won't do it.'

Bemused, for he had so frequently made generous offers
of financial assistance over the years, Prudence frowned.
'Then…what will you do?'

'This is painful,' Nik told her drily. 'Let me be frank. Unless you agree to stay as my wife, I won't do anything.'

In shock, Prudence stared across the room at him. 'You
don't mean that…'

'This is why I refuse to criticise Theo…we are both strong
men who like our own way and we don't do failure well.'

'Nik…you're not like my grandfather.'

'I'm willing to employ pressure and coercion to make you
do what I want,' Nik pointed out drily.

Prudence shook her head slowly, surely. 'No, you
wouldn't…'

Chilling dark eyes met hers with unflinching challenge.
'What would you know? You've never crossed me before. I
told you that I didn't want a divorce.'

'I've always been able to depend on you,' Prudence reminded him doggedly.

'Not this time. Our interests are in conflict—'

'What about Dottie and Sam?'

Nik executed a tiny fluid shrug and surveyed her steadily.

'All the animals?' Prudence asked with shattered incredulity. 'Many of them are too old or difficult to be rehomed.'

'I know.'

'You would sacrifice the animals?'

'No, you will. There will be no sacrifices if you decide to
remain my wife.'

Prudence lifted her hand and raked her fingers through

the heavy fall of her chestnut-brown hair. Her hand was not quite steady. She was starting to recall the reality that she had never managed to match Nik's public image with the male she knew privately. Or the male that she *believed* that she had known and understood. He was quite correct: she had never crossed him—well, not until she had asked for a divorce that he did not want. His ruthless reputation in business was legendary. He was not exactly a pussycat with the other women in his life either. He might have treated her and the women in his family with indulgence, but beyond that select circle Nik was most famous for being cold and unfeeling.

She clenched her hands tight. 'I owe Dottie and Sam a lot. I promised them a secure home, and Sam's health will suffer if he's subjected to more stress. And although the animals here might not be human beings…if anything was to happen to them I think I would die of guilt and a broken heart…'

'So stop fighting me and every little problem will vanish,' Nik advised softly. 'As long as you are my wife, I will take care of you and your enemies will be mine.'

Gooseflesh prickled at the nape of her neck. His eyes were as dark as windows at night, his dark, rich drawl strikingly detached. She fought off the hollow sensation of fear in her belly. 'I could put off the divorce—'

'No, all or nothing—'

'Well, it wouldn't matter now whether I divorced you or not, would it?' Prudence threw back with a bitterness that was new to her experience. 'I'm certainly not going to be having a child without some degree of financial stability. I hope I have more sense. If I drop the divorce, will you be satisfied? Will you loan me the money then?'

'All or nothing,' Nik reminded her lazily. 'I want my wife in my bed, where she belongs…'

Her cheeks fired pink. Her hands screwed up into fists. She regarded him with furious disbelief. 'Rot in hell!'

His lush black lashes were low over his stunning dark golden eyes. 'I'm an old-fashioned guy,' he murmured with insolent cool. 'I'd have had you there a lot sooner, had I known that the wedding night was a non-event.'

'It was too late even then—'

'I don't think so. I'm told I have remarkable powers of persuasion. Had I not been haunted by the fear that I had put myself beyond the pale, you wouldn't have been calling the independent shots all these years,' Nik delivered, lean, powerful features stamped with forbidding strength. 'You're my wife and I have never thought of you as anything else—'

'A poor thing…but my own?' she misquoted hotly.

'Mine…that's the one part you got right. What is mine stays mine—'

'I will not be your wife…*ever*!'

'Your decision.' Nik strolled out of the room and it was a split-second before Prudence unfroze and chased after him.

'You can't leave me like this!' she wailed.

Nik tilted his arrogant dark head back, brilliant eyes gleaming. 'I can do whatever I want to do.'

'If you don't take back what you've suggested, I'll never forgive you for it…'

'That's a risk I'm prepared to take.'

'I could take you to court and claim alimony from you, and you would be forced to give me some financial help,' she protested.

'But the legal process would move very, very slowly and you don't have the time to wait,' Nik countered with cool clarity.

Her shoulders slumped. 'So you think it's OK to kick me when I'm already down?'

Ice in his hard gaze, Nik studied her, his beautifully sculpted mouth grim. 'You're the only woman I've ever asked to marry me. To listen to you speak of our marriage as though it is some form of abuse is intolerable. I treated you with honour—'

'This is not honour I'm dealing with!'

Nik reached into his pocket and withdrew a piece of paper. He tossed it down on the hall table. 'If you want to be treated with honour, behave like a wife!' he launched at her lethally.

Prudence stared down, transfixed, at the newspaper photo of her with Leo in the London restaurant. That snatched picture had actually appeared in print? Leo would be equally appalled by that development. She was astonished, too, at how misleading an impression a photo could give. There she was, seemingly holding hands with Leo, and her tears were not visible. She simply appeared to be looking at her companion with intense interest. Her lips parted on the hail of words that would have assured Nik that Leo was truly only a friend. Then she remembered the scrapbooks of Nik's love affairs and her heart hardened to the consistency of a granite rock. Folding her lush mouth firmly shut, she said nothing. So Nik didn't like it when the tables were turned? Tough!

Nik waited for her to utter a denial and an explanation. He knew she would not lie to him. When the rushing silence continued, he felt strangely light-headed and hollow and thinking was suddenly a challenge. And then *bang*, those weird sensations were gone, and in their place was a primitive corrosive anger that made it impossible for him even to look at her.

'You have twenty-four hours to make a decision—'

'Twenty-four hours?' she echoed in consternation.

'You don't understand, do you?' Nik swung lithely back to face her again, lean, strong face hard with resolve, dark eyes chilling. 'Even if I come to the rescue, Craighill Farm will no longer be your home. You can't stay here.'

Prudence frowned uncertainly. 'Even if you come to the rescue? But you *said*—'

'Think it through.' His dark drawl was abrasive. 'Theo will not let me buy this place for you. He'll be waiting for me to try. He won't sell to me and he's too devious to fall for a fake buyer. I have to find you and your dependants somewhere else to live.'

Prudence was struggling to get her head around the extremely unpalatable facts he was spelling out. 'Somewhere else? For *all* of us?' she exclaimed. 'But that would be impossible—'

'A tall order in this time-frame, but not impossible. If I throw enough money and personnel at the problem, I can do it. I will do it for you.'

Disturbingly conscious of his sheer height and breadth, Prudence was very tense. He was so close she could have touched him and she was appalled by the strength of her craving to do exactly that. She had suffered too many shocks recently, and at the back of her mind had still dwelt the comforting conviction that Nik would pull off a miracle and make everything perfect again. Now he was telling her that no, that wasn't possible and the situation was even worse than she appreciated. Even with his support she would still have to move out of Craighill Farm. Her head was starting to ache, pointless thoughts whirling round in ever-decreasing circles. But one thought remained crystal-clear.

'If you force me to be your wife on those terms, you'll lose my trust forever,' she warned him fiercely.

Nik rested dark golden eyes of challenge on her. 'Sometimes there isn't a choice. Just as this is the only way I have of ensuring that our marriage has a future. You now know that you'll accept my offer, because it's the only one on the table.'

Prudence studied the wall and trembled with temper and resentment. But she gritted her teeth together to bite back hasty words of defiance. As usual he was right on target. He *was* her only option and there was no time to waste.

'All right, so for what it's worth and even though it's very hard to see what you could possibly get out of such an arrangement…I'll…be…your…wife.' Forced out, her gritty words of surrender ricocheted off her tongue like individual bullets.

His big, powerful frame tensing at the return of that strange light-headed sensation, Nik was startled into questioning if he had caught some virus. His eyes narrowing, he kept his entire attention pinned to her and breathed in slow and deep. 'You will never regret it.'

'I hate you now…is that really what you want?'

Nik cast a flashing glance through the open doorway behind her through which he could see the crisp white and pink linen on her bed. His taut body throbbed with sexual heat and hunger: he knew exactly what he wanted. She didn't hate him, she *couldn't* hate him; he refused to accept that. His smouldering dark golden gaze shimmied down over her mutinous face to rest on her luscious mouth, then travelled from there to the tantalising fullness of her pouting breasts, where he lingered before passing on with assurance to the highly feminine swell of her hips below her small waist.

'Don't you dare look me over like I'm something on a butcher's block!' Prudence launched at him in a tempest of fury and mortification.

'You're my wife…it's allowed. I also now know what a fantastic body you work so hard to hide beneath those clothes. I want you and I'm not ashamed to admit it.' Nik scored a lean forefinger along the ripe curve of her lower lip and watched her shiver as though she were standing up to storm-force winds. 'How long are you planning to make me wait?'

Prudence reddened to the roots of her hair. On a level she was reluctant to explore she was sinfully willing to hear that she could be an ongoing object of desire for him. 'Stop it,' she told him primly.

'I can't.'

Prudence could feel her own weakness rising like a tide inside her. She wanted him, too, she acknowledged; she wanted him to an indecent degree. Rage and self-loathing tearing at her like vengeful claws, Prudence dragged her gaze from the earthy desire in his, forced her trembling legs to move in the direction of the door and then yanked it open. 'I will start behaving as a wife when I am in my new home and not before then.'

'You're kidding me…' Nik breathed in a raw undertone of rampant incredulity.

Prudence could feel something that felt uncommonly like a power current leaping through her. He really did lust after her, she conceded in astonishment. It was incomprehensible to her, but the high-voltage charge of his white-hot sexuality was focused on her like a blowtorch. He wasn't used to anything other than instant gratification either. Waiting would indeed be a new and challenging experience for him.

Prudence drew herself up to her full insignificant height, feeling very much taller than she usually did. 'No, I'm not kidding you.'

Nik surveyed her with smouldering disbelief. 'We made a deal—'

'When you've fulfilled your part of the bargain by finding us all somewhere else to live, I will fulfil mine,' Prudence stated tautly.

His strong jaw line hardened. 'Do you doubt my ability to keep my promise?'

Prudence jerked a stiff shoulder. 'No, but I'm being forced into this and I won't pretend otherwise. I won't behave like your wife until I have to. I don't even feel married—'

'But you will, I assure you,' Nik sliced in, soft and low and lethal, his Greek accent feathering over every syllable with purring exactitude. 'Give me time.'

In shock at the agreement she had given, Prudence stared into space for a long time after he had gone. That was that, then. She was finally going to get to be Mrs Angelis years after she had stopped weaving dreams round the idea. This time around, however, she had few illusions. Even so, the discovery that Theo Demakis and Nik Angelis were brothers under the skin had shattered Prudence. Only now was it dawning on her that Nik must always have been tough and unemotional. Indeed, those very qualities might well have persuaded her grandfather that Nik Angelis would make the right kind of son-in-law. She had just learnt the hard way that, when it came to getting what he wanted, Nik was as ruthless and cold-blooded as his reputation implied.

But perhaps Nik needed to learn that a wife was not as easily controlled as an employee or an inanimate object, she reflected tautly. Perhaps he needed to learn that she could fight back and be every bit as strong and dispassionate as any man could be. In fact, if she played her cards right, Nik might even be glad to give her a divorce by the time she had finished with him…

Leo hurried in at tea time to brandish the offending newspaper photo before her eyes. 'Have you seen this? I was gobsmacked when some pupils I teach showed it to me and asked if that was me,' he groaned. 'Goodness knows what Stella will think! Did you get your loan?'

'Nik and I have decided to try being married for a while,' Prudence informed him as casually as she could.

Leo was not taken in. 'I don't believe you. He's the Casanova of his generation. How can a woman with your moral views *try* being married to a bloke with three mistresses?'

Eyes veiled, Prudence jerked a noncommittal shoulder. Leo might be a close friend but some plans weren't for sharing. She was planning to fight Nik from behind the scenes and he would eventually discover that she could get down and dirty, too. If he could use blackmail, she could use female cunning. Had it ever occurred to Nik that they did not have a pre-nuptial agreement that might protect his wealth in the event of a divorce? She thought not, for Nik was too well accustomed to her fierce independence and her long-standing refusal to benefit financially from their relationship. Well, she was about to change tack. If Nik was unfaithful to her she would hire the best divorce lawyer in London. And at the end of it all, every animal in the sanctuary would be able to look forward to a lifetime of clover and honey…

CHAPTER FIVE

THE LIMOUSINE PURRED down a long wooded drive and paused at the crown of a gentle hill. It was the perfect vantage point for a view of the ancient property that sat at the heart of the lush green parkland.

As the sole occupant of the limo, Prudence, who had come out determined not to be impressed, discovered that she was being impressed to death. She had never taken much interest in houses, but then she had never seen a house quite like Oakmere Abbey before. A hotchpotch of different roof heights and wonderfully tall chimneys, matched with mellow stone and mullioned windows, gave it a beauty and warmth that she found amazingly appealing.

The car phone buzzed and she answered it.

'First impressions?' Nik asked lazily, his rich, dark drawl setting up a vibration down her responsive spine.

Prudence was not prepared to gush. 'It certainly enjoys a lovely setting.'

'Look, the board meeting overran. I'm still an hour away. Why don't you check out the land and the agricultural buildings first? We'll view the abbey together.'

The chauffeur, evidently already primed with his instructions, ferried her to a remarkably well-kept farm yard, where the estate manager was waiting to give her a guided tour. It was only a week since Nik had promised to find a new home for the sanctuary and, although he had admitted that old buildings held little appeal for him, the abbey met what he deemed to be the most important requirements. Within reach of London and currently empty, it offered ample land and livestock housing as well as staff apartments and cottages.

Nik, accustomed to women who never put him to the trouble of having to find them, finally ran Prudence to earth in the stable yard at the back of the house. Chesnut-brown hair ruffling in the breeze, one hand dug in the pocket of an over-large weathered green waxed jacket that might have been new a decade ago, she was seated on a bale of hay in an open shed, cheerfully chatting to the middle-aged estate manager and petting a dog. Animated and laughing, she looked amazingly attractive and full of life. Then she saw Nik and instantly her oval face tensed and her lovely natural smile dropped away. It made him feel like the guy who stole Christmas.

Having greeted the older man, Nik extended a lean brown hand to Prudence in an intimate gesture, as calculated as it was determined to make her accept the change in their relationship. 'Let's go and see the house…I told the agent we'd prefer to look it over alone.'

Scrambling off the bale, Prudence wondered morosely if she would ever overcome the breathlessness and racing heartbeat that Nik's sudden appearance could always inspire. Every time she saw him his lean, dark, bronzed face made something tender twist and ache inside her. He was gorgeous, he had always been gorgeous, but he also rejoiced in an extra-special and very powerful something that made her eyes want to cling…and cling…and cling. Dragging her attention from him, she knew that if she didn't learn to get a grip on her reaction to his sleek, darkly handsome looks, she would humiliate herself and suffer a great deal of unnecessary pain. She ignored his hand altogether and buried her own uncomfortably in her pockets. Passive resistance, she reminded herself, no unnecessary physical contact of any description. She had to be careful. If she gave him the slightest encouragement or allowed the smallest intimacy, he'd take advantage. His intellect had programmed him to take advantage of weak and foolish opponents. Look what he was already doing to her peace of mind! If she didn't watch out and keep him at a distance, he'd soon be shaking a hoop in front of her and snapping his fingers to make her jump!

'Your thoughts so far?' Nik prompted flatly, aware of her unease in his presence and infuriated by it. Her warmth and trusting openness had vanished. What was the matter with her? So he had put pressure on her to give their marriage a chance. He was willing to make the effort, why wasn't she? She had to be in love with Leo Burleigh.

'There's a lot of land...the sanctuary would only use a small part of it,' Prudence commented. 'An estate this size must cost an absolute fortune.'

'I can afford it. The location couldn't be bettered.'

In a silence that fairly bristled with edgy undertones, they walked round to the main entrance. The great hall rejoiced in elaborate carved screens and a flagstoned floor. Nik frowned. 'It'll be very cold in winter.'

Prudence was admiring the grand stone chimney piece that was incised with a date in the sixteenth century. 'Too much heat isn't healthy,' she told him, walking past him to explore a vast reception room that looked across the park to the beautiful woods in the distance. 'That view is out of this world. It's like the twenty-first century doesn't exist.'

Nik, who was rather attached to the twenty-first century and all the technology that went with it, knew when to keep quiet. Prudence, who was shying away if her shadow so much as encountered his, was, he soon noticed, getting very touchy feely with her ancient surroundings. Rooms tacked on without any apparent regard to the architectural whole were pronounced 'charming' and the innumerable opportunities to burn open fires in giant smoke-blackened hearths praised to the skies. She termed the horrendous basic barn of a kitchen 'characterful', informed him that the need to provide heating, rewiring and plumbing was 'to be expected', went into raptures over panelled rooms that all looked the gloomy same to him and saw nothing amiss with the serious lack of bathrooms.

'My goodness…the master bedroom even has an *en suite*!' Prudence exclaimed, looking madly impressed by the sight of the giant roll-top bath that lurked in an alcove, complete with a Victorian enamelled shower frame. 'Isn't that just amazing?'

Nik surveyed the elderly fixtures: 'amazing' was not the word that came to his mind. He was frankly appalled. In his opinion everything they had seen belonged in a builder's skip. His apartment rejoiced in a pool, a hot tub and a sauna; the bathrooms came equipped with power showers, wet rooms, steam facilities and spa baths. He could not imagine living any other way.

'The abbey is smaller than I appreciated,' Nik remarked. 'It needs a major extension. But this is a listed building and it would be a headache getting plans passed for one.'

Paying no great heed to his comments, Prudence reluctantly removed her admiring gaze from the bath and strolled back into the dusty corridor. 'I think a dozen bedrooms is more than adequate. But if you felt it wasn't, there's a very pretty courtyard of what used to be staff accommodation at the rear. It could easily be made accessible from the main house.'

The suggestion left his lean, strong face unmoved. 'The condition of the house is also a good deal rougher than I was led to expect.'

Beneath his bemused gaze, Prudence, who seemed blissfully unaware of his negative outlook on the abbey, caressed a carved wooden panel with reverent fingertips. 'I suppose it does need a little updating here and there—'

'Here and there?' Nik echoed in disbelief. 'I don't think it's been touched since the nineteen-twenties!'

'Which is marvellous, because it's completely unspoilt.' Prudence sent a dreamy smile in his general direction. 'It's been a happy house, too…I can feel it in my bones.'

In the act of adding another nought to what he believed Oakmere would ultimately cost him, Nik registered that she was finally smiling at him again and he studied her with veiled intensity. 'Would you like to live here?'

'Oh, yes…' Prudence had no doubts whatsoever on that score.

She had walked into the great hall and it had been a case of love at first sight. Her only previous experience of so sudden and intense an attachment had been falling in love with Nik eight years earlier. That had been, she was willing to admit, a most unhappy experience. Fortunately, she was convinced that loving bricks and mortar would be much safer and more rewarding. She was well aware that Oakmere wasn't Nik's style. He was accustomed to luxury and very contemporary in his tastes. He had also never evinced an interest in historic buildings or in country life. But those realities didn't bother Prudence in the slightest. After all, she reflected resolutely, the abbey would ultimately be her house, her home, as she had every intention of claiming it as part of the divorce settlement when they broke up.

Nik watched the flutter of her curling eyelashes lift on her blue eyes. That she really went for the house filled him with intense satisfaction. He had picked a winner. He watched her gently pat the balustrade on the staircase as if it were a living thing in need of affection and he almost laughed: she was the most tender-hearted, truly feminine woman he had ever known.

Her preoccupied gaze roused his curiosity. 'What are you thinking about?'

Disconcerted pink warmed her cheeks. 'Nothing important—'

A slow burning smile slashed his handsome mouth. 'I bet you were thinking about us…living here, *pethi mou.*'

Even though instant guilt flared through her when he made that assumption, that smile of his made a curl of heat leap and dance in the pit of her tummy. Simultaneously, the thoughts in her head burned to dust. 'Maybe…'

The silence lay thick. She met brilliant dark golden eyes and was suddenly impossibly aware of every inch of her all too female body and of every tiny breath that she drew. She straightened her back in an effort to ease the tingling sensitivity of her breasts.

Bracing long brown fingers on the wall to one side of her head, Nik angled his proud dark head down to press a light, teasing kiss to the corner of her mouth. With a low-pitched gasp, she turned her head to blindly seek more direct contact. His breath fanning her cheek, he toyed with the soft fullness of her lower lip, rimming the upper with an erotic dart of his tongue. 'Nik…' She leant forward, literally begging for more, her entire being on fire for the taste of his passionate mouth on hers.

'Mr Angelis?' A male voice called from the direction of the great hall.

Startled back to reality, Prudence jerked back from Nik as if she had been violently slapped.

'Relax, it's only the agent,' Nik breathed with a husky sound of amusement. 'Come home with me.'

Beetroot-pink, Prudence retorted, 'You can forget that!' and hurried off to greet the agent.

Nik raked impatient fingers through his luxuriant black hair and expelled his breath on a hiss. He had coerced her into accepting his terms and he had expected too much too soon. But his bewilderment lingered for the Prudence he had believed he knew inside out, who was gentle, soft-hearted and serene. The woman he was currently dealing with was passionate, stubborn and angry to a degree he would not have believed.

The rich scent of the roses in her exquisite bouquet made Prudence breathe in deeply. Yet her brow had an anxious furrow and her eyes were strained.

In a couple of hours she would be walking out of Craighill Farm forever and taking up residence at Oakmere Abbey as Nik's wife. From then on, Nik, and the marriage that he had sworn he wanted to be a real one, would be on trial. If he betrayed her trust their marriage would be over. She had to fight her own corner, stand up for what she believed in. No wilting wallflower would ever be the equal of Nik Angelis, and she could not make the mistake of getting emotionally involved with him again. An unfaithful husband, who broke her heart and humiliated her, would never make her happy, she acknowledged ruefully. For that same reason she had visited her doctor and had embarked on a course of contraceptive pills. She would not run the risk of falling pregnant in a marriage that might not last that long.

Nik had forced her into a marriage that she wanted to put behind her. Yet, in recent weeks, Nik could not have been more considerate or helpful. Although she had not seen him once in the flesh, he had phoned every day and had gone to remarkable lengths to ensure that she had practical assistance in every corner of her life. For starters, professionals had taken care of all the work of moving for her. Dottie and Sam were over the moon with the cottage they had been offered and were already installed in it. Over the past three days all the animals had been transferred and settled on the abbey estate and a full-time worker had been engaged for the sanctuary.

Nik had even sent her an outfit to wear. He knew she hated shopping and had probably assumed that she would be grateful to be relieved of the task. But Prudence was not pleased at all. Nik buying clothes for her only reminded her that he was a notorious womaniser, who knew more about female garments and sizes than she thought decent or acceptable.

That awareness in mind, Prudence pulled a face at the opulent, long halter-neck dress and bolero jacket hanging on the back of the door. It was definitely not her style. It was obvious, though, that Nik was determined to behave as though the day was a special occasion. The outfit might also be a hefty hint that some sort of surprise party was to take place. She could only cringe at the potential prospect of once again greeting Nik's friends and relations in a dress that bore more than a passing resemblance to a wedding gown. The white silk sheath might be considerably more elegant and sophisticated than the frilly satin horror she had worn at nineteen, but it had heavy bridal overtones.

As she climbed into the limousine sent to collect her, the removal company arrived to pack up her last possessions. There was a selection of magazines in the car and she leafed through a fashion publication without much interest, until a glimpse of a familiar face made her freeze. It was Cassia Morikis, who had put her talent for acting to good use as a soap star on television before her marriage to a British rock star. His recent death and the subsequent fight over his estate by his previous wives and children had caused more than a few headlines. Prudence studied Cassia's exquisite face and held the page up to the light to see if she could spot a single flaw. But she was disappointed: Cassia was still incredibly beautiful.

The blonde's spite did not show on the surface, Prudence conceded ruefully. On the day that Prudence had married Nik, Cassia had upstaged her at every turn. Cassia had worn white as well and had inevitably looked much better in it. Everyone had also known that Cassia had been Nik's girlfriend a month earlier and she had enjoyed the support of a sympathetic and attentive band of friends.

'What a big girl you are in every department, Pudding,' Cassia had whispered in her saccharine-sweet voice to Prudence when nobody else was listening. 'Poor Nik won't be able to close his eyes and pretend that it's me in bed with him tonight!'

'Stop it,' Prudence had urged in a stricken undertone.

'No, stopping is the one thing Nik and I *won't* be doing. Enjoy your wedding ring. It's the most you'll ever have of him.' Cassia had given her a malicious smile. 'Why do you think you're not getting a honeymoon? Nik refused to do without me for that long.'

Reliving that poisonous memory from the past, Prudence shivered. Cassia had soon underlined her threats with a wounding demonstration of her hold on Nik. When Prudence had noticed that Nik was missing, she had not wanted to believe that she would find him with the beautiful blonde. Any faith she had had in her bridegroom had come crashing down when she saw him in Cassia's arms. Yet Prudence was willing to concede that the explanation Nik had given her just weeks ago might well be true. Perhaps Cassia had been the schemer and the instigator; perhaps Nik had rejected the girl's advances. Unfortunately, Prudence had not stayed around long enough to find out either way.

The limo finally drew up outside Oakmere Abbey, and Prudence stepped out onto a red carpet that ran all the way to the front door. For a split-second she felt a little dizzy and she blinked in surprise but the moment was almost immediately forgotten in her eagerness to see what had been done with the house. A week ago, Nik had thrown an army of cleaners and decorators into the abbey to make a select few rooms habitable. While he had insisted that he wanted to surprise her, she had worried that he might allow the atmosphere of the house to be spoilt with inappropriate colour schemes and furnishings.

The front door stood wide open. She wandered in slowly and immediately smiled when she saw the fire burning in the chilly great hall. A glorious flower arrangement stood on a table and a couple of comfortable antique chairs added to the welcoming ambience.

'What do you think?' Nik prompted.

She whirled round, her dress rustling round her legs in a white swirl of silk, and saw Nik in the shadows by the wall. Light from the leaded windows burnished his black hair and lean, dark, devastating face. Her mouth ran dry and she snatched in a jerky breath. 'I…I—'

'You look wonderful in that dress,' Nik cut in, stunning dark golden eyes travelling over her as thoroughly as a coating of molten honey.

Prudence tensed. 'You don't need to say stuff like that…'

'I do and you need to listen.' Nik closed a determined hand over hers and tugged her over to the mirror on the opposite wall. 'You have to learn to see what I see—'

Prudence squeezed her eyes tight shut, chin taking on a mutinous angle. 'No, I don't. I've never liked flattery.'

Nik pulled her back into the hard, muscular heat of his lithe, powerful frame. 'It's not flattery…for the first time ever you are wearing something that fits your divine shape!'

Prudence had to open her eyes to roll them and express how unimpressed she was by that compliment. 'My shape is not—'

The dark golden eyes above her head blazed with fierce impatience. 'Do you know why I didn't like your mother? She got a kick out of running you down and telling you how plain you were! But look at your face, your bone structure…and all that glorious hair!'

Dumbfounded by that speech, Prudence opened and closed her mouth a couple of times and stared at his reflection.

'You also have a body to die for,' he informed her, lean brown hands sliding up to cup the sides of her full breasts in a manner that shook her. 'I love it.'

'Really…?' Prudence squeaked, watching as though mesmerised while his sure hands slide down her taut ribcage to rest at her small waist for a moment before skimming down to shape the voluptuous swell of her hips.

'Can't you tell?' Nik splayed long fingers across her midriff to ease her back into closer connection with his blatant arousal.

Hot colour warmed her cheeks while a secret surge of tremendously feminine satisfaction engulfed her.

'If I say you're sexy…you're sexy,' Nik husked, letting his lips tease a trail down the side of her neck until she quivered in response. 'But right now, we have something rather more important to attend to and I have to cool it. In the room next door the priest who conducted our wedding eight years ago is waiting to bless our marriage.'

Already bemused by that heated little interlude and with her legs still feeling distinctly wobbly, Prudence was even more disconcerted by that announcement. 'I beg your pardon?'

'You said you didn't feel married to me…I thought that the blessing might improve that situation.'

Assailed by several hostile reactions, not one of which she was willing to share with him, Prudence buttoned her lips and studied the ancient flagstones with furious intensity. Imagine Nik going to such outrageously traditional lengths to impress her! Imagine the nerve of a guy who had used virtual blackmail to keep her in the marriage then daring to request a blessing to ratify that act!

'It's my way of demonstrating that I'm committed to making our marriage work,' Nik imparted without a shade of remorse or embarrassment.

'But I'm not,' Prudence confided with helpless honesty.

Nik surveyed her with glittering dark eyes and an aggressive set to his hard jaw line. 'Given time, you *will* be…'

Prudence said nothing because it did not feel like the moment or the place to argue the point. The venerable old priest, Father Vasos, greeted them with pleasure. Sincerity shone from him and struck a chord within Prudence that made her squirm. How could she receive a blessing with a heart that was already closed to the words that would be spoken? How could she continue to deny the fact that she still loved Nik to distraction? Would it be so foolish to give Nik one more chance? When Nik eased a new wedding ring on her bare finger, her throat convulsed with sudden emotion. By the time Father Vasos left, her thoughts were in turmoil and her resolve to fight Nik by whatever means were available had been badly shaken.

Nik showed her into another room where a table had been set with crisp linen and gleaming silver. 'Just for the two of us?'

'Three or more is company and I want you all to myself.'

'Who's cooking?' She was determined not to betray her astonishment at the elaborate arrangements he had made to mark the day as a very special event.

'I flew in a chef from Paris. This time, I want everything to be perfect, *glikia mou*,' Nik told her without hesitation. 'You deserve only the best.'

Candles were lit by staff as silent and discreet as shadows. The food was delicious. She nibbled at the various dishes, listening to the melodious rise and fall of Nik's dark, sexy drawl, acknowledging that he was wonderfully entertaining company. Every so often she would treat herself to a single appreciative look at his hard, bronzed features, his dazzling eyes and beautifully shaped mouth. Her heartbeat would race and she would address her attention to her food again and scold herself for letting her mind wander like a dreaming schoolgirl.

Next her attention would stray to her shiny new wedding ring. That had been a surprisingly sensitive and much appreciated gift, because it was years since she had left her original rings behind in Athens. When she studied the slender platinum band, her hard-earned cynicism threatened to desert her and she would wonder if a leopard could change his spots and turn into a faithful husband, keen to embrace home, hearth and family.

'Have you had enough to eat?' Nik enquired lazily.

Prudence nodded, almost afraid to speak lest she somehow destroy the enchanted spell that had enfolded her.

Springing upright, he reached for her hand and she gave it to him without thinking about it.

'Now we dance…'

Prudence just laughed as he escorted her out of the room. 'How can we dance?'

And then she heard the music. The evocative notes were cascading down from behind the carved screens above the great hall and the furniture had been set back by the wall. She met Nik's amused gaze and exclaimed in astonishment, 'There are musicians up there?'

'Playing just for us.' Enclosing her in his arms, Nik whirled her round before she could catch her breath. 'Eight years ago, you refused even to dance with me.'

Prudence winced. 'I was too self-conscious to get up in front of all the wedding guests. But you only asked me once—'

'Playing it cool was all I had left. I was still a boy and my pride was hurting,' Nik countered wryly. 'Your grandfather had bought you a husband and everyone knew it—'

'Oh, no, Nik…surely you can't have been thinking like that? You didn't have any more choice than I had!'

'Friends told me how lucky I was to catch a real live heiress. After all, Theo was and is richer than Croesus and my spendthrift father was on the brink of bankruptcy. I felt like the money meant that you owned me body and soul and I hated it,' Nik admitted bluntly, wondering why she should be so honest in other ways and yet should still feel the need to pretend that she had not had a choice about whether or not she married him. 'I wasn't happy until I could repay every penny.'

Prudence was aghast. 'No…no,' she protested, taken aback by what he was admitting, for it had not occurred to her to see that angle before. 'I would've died if I'd known you felt like that—'

'But I did feel like that, *pethi mou*.' Nik looked down at her with rueful regret.

'Too much pride,' she scolded uncomfortably.

'Maybe. Certainly, when Theo told me last month that he

was cutting you out of his will, I was relieved. It sets us both free of his interference for good.'

'Hmm…' Prudence was revelling in the skill with which he was whirling her round the room in perfect time to the music. She was dancing on air in the arms of the guy of her dreams. 'I so wish our wedding had been like this.'

'That's the whole idea. This is how it *should* have been,' Nik asserted, angling his sleek dark head down to kiss her.

Her body gave a leap of almost painful tension and response went zipping through her in a fireball of energy.

'That was off the schedule. I'm aiming at perfection this time,' Nik confided. 'We still have to cut the cake, drink the champagne—'

Prudence gripped his lapels, stretched up on tiptoes and whispered feverishly, 'We could take the cake and champagne up to bed with us…'

Nik tensed in surprise and dealt her an arrested glance. 'Prudence Angelis…what's come over you?'

Prudence pressed her hot face into his suit jacket, drinking in the familiar scent of him with sensually appreciative pleasure. She felt weak with wanting. 'I don't know, but if your aim is perfection it could be a mistake to stick too closely to the schedule…'

Nik vented an earthy laugh of appreciation and swept her out of the room without further ado.

CHAPTER SIX

ON THE THRESHOLD of the master bedroom, Nik scooped Prudence up into his arms and carried her in. He settled her down on the four-poster bed. She lay back and kicked off her shoes, her deeply appreciative eyes sparkling at the elaborate canopy above her and the beautiful rose-strewn curtains hanging at each corner. 'This is my dream come true. All my life I've wanted a bed like this…how did you guess?'

'Your girlie bedroom spoke for you. You're a romantic.'

At that label, Prudence stiffened, wrinkled her nose and sat up on her knees. 'No, I'm not.'

Amused dark eyes rested on her. 'It's not a crime.'

Her curling lashes hid her expression but the angle of her chin had a firmness that spoke for her.

'You're very wary,' Nik drawled. 'Can't you trust me?'

Prudence shook her head.

Nik was taken aback by the speed of that response. 'But you must trust me to some extent.'

Prudence shook her head a second time.

Nik levelled censorious golden eyes on her. 'That is outrageous…you're my wife!'

'Let's not forget why I'm here today.'

His gaze shimmered like a heatwave. 'I'm fighting for our marriage…why can't you appreciate that?'

'Maybe I don't like your methods.'

'Some day you'll look back and be glad I fought for you, *pethi mou*,' Nik declared with fierce assurance.

'So you think you've been fighting for me?' Prudence was shaken by the obvious strength of his conviction in that fact. She could see that the secret of his phenomenal success lay in his outlook. When blackmail could be presented as an act of heroism and matrimonial devotion, how could she help but be impressed?

Nik flung back his arrogant dark head. 'What else?'

'But you still haven't explained why you've gone to so much effort,' she pointed out gently.

Nik sent her a winging look of frustration as if he could not comprehend why that should seem a mystery to her. 'You're my wife. What other reason do I need?'

Prudence lifted and dropped her shoulders for if he had no idea why, she had even less.

'Did you enjoy today?' he asked huskily.

Meeting his stunning dark golden eyes, she felt a sensation like her heart lurching inside her: he was that beautiful. 'Much more than our wedding day…'

'The night will be spectacular,' he promised, leaning down to tip the bolero jacket off her shoulders and slide it off.

All of a sudden her agile brain stopped racing and throwing thoughts at her faster than she could handle. She connected with smouldering dark golden eyes and breathing became a considerable challenge. Simply by looking at her, Nik could plunge her into a state of hopeless desire. In an effort to overcome that sense of weakness, Prudence tugged him down to her and began to unknot his tie.

'I like this sudden need to rip my clothes off,' Nik confided, hot eyes melded to her.

Although her face was burning, Prudence had not lost her resolve. Rising onto her knees, she helped him out of his jacket and embarked on his shirt buttons with fingers that felt mortifyingly clumsy. 'But maybe it's a little less practised than what you're used to—'

Disconcerted by that comment, Nik closed his hand over hers. 'Don't undervalue what I have with you. This is different for me.'

Wanting to believe that but afraid to, Prudence hesitated momentarily. 'Is it?'

'Of course it is…' Nik covered her lips with an unexpected tenderness.

His tongue delved into the moist cavern of her mouth and sensual anticipation took her by storm. Suddenly the hunger he had taught her to feel, and which she had suppressed with every atom of her considerable will-power, was in the ascendant again. She was shocked by the urgency of her craving. The skilled movement of his mouth on hers, the explicit intrusion of his tongue were enough to make her shake and shiver as though she had a fever. One kiss ran hotly into the next.

A dark flush scoring his hard cheekbones, stunning eyes glittering, Nik undid the halter-neck of her dress and slowly drew the opulent fabric down to release her full curves from the shaped bodice.

'You're gorgeous,' he said thickly.

Entranced by her creamy breasts and the distended rosy buds awaiting his attention, he pressed her back against the pillows. Smoothly extracting her from the gown round her hips, he tossed it aside. He bent over her with a husky sound of satisfaction to let his lips toy with a pouting pink nipple. Heat burst low in her pelvis and tensed her hips and an ache that was almost painful began to stir.

'You're also very clever,' Nik murmured intently as he dragged himself back from her with flattering reluctance to shed his clothes.

'Am I?' Her body was taut and heavy with the sensuality he had awakened and she found it an effort to string even those two words together. With his amazing eyes fired to scorching gold and his shirt hanging loose on a brown, hair-roughened expanse of muscular chest, Nik also looked utterly breathtaking.

He gave her a slashing grin of masculine appreciation. 'You said no…you made me wait. I'm not used to practising patience, but there has been an unexpected benefit—I haven't been this excited since I was a teenager.'

Embarrassment at his candour and satisfaction mingled within Prudence, before she picked up on the much more important fact he had just given her: he had not allowed any other woman to assuage his hot-blooded libido. As there were always sexually available women within reach of rich powerful tycoons, this could only mean that Nik had made a new and conscious choice to be faithful to his wife. Happiness thrilled through Prudence. For the first time it occurred to her that, if she set the marital bars high enough, his natural need to compete, excel and win might actually make him strive to meet her expectations.

'I wasn't thinking of that angle,' Prudence muttered honestly, self-conscious but trying to smile rather than act the prude.

'I've thought of you from every angle, *thespinis mou*,' Nik confessed, strolling back to join her, unashamedly naked and brazenly aroused.

He had called her his woman and she wondered if she could be. Because, if she set her pride aside, it was what she had always wanted, indeed all she had ever dreamt of. And for that chance she was still willing to put her pride on the line, she acknowledged, her mouth running dry as he came down beside her on the bed. He was as lithe and powerful in his masculine beauty as a pagan god.

'Nik,' she whispered below the passionate onslaught of his hungry mouth, fingers spreading against the warm, muscular wall of his hard torso. 'When I look at you—'

'Don't just look…*touch*,' Nik urged, hungry golden eyes striking hers as he carried her hand down over his flat stomach to the aggressive jut of his bold erection.

Involuntarily she froze. 'I don't know how—'

'But I know…' a provocative smile slashed his handsome mouth '…and I intend to enjoy teaching you.'

It had never occurred to her that picking up fresh skills could be so stimulating. Or so empowering. She was absorbed by the delight of that new intimacy. The right to touch and explore Nik, the challenge of pushing him to the edge of his self-control, was utterly seductive.

When he swore quietly and wrenched himself back from her, his hot golden gaze ablaze with passion, she could see how hard he had found it to rein back his libido. His big, powerful body was covered in a fine sheen of sweat, his muscles were knotted and he was trembling. He was breathing fast and shallowly.

'Enough…'

'Spoilsport…' Prudence gave him a languorous glance and slowly she smiled, her own body tingling with sensual awareness. The next time she would fine-tune her technique, she reflected with newly learnt confidence.

Sheer bewilderment gripped Nik. She was lounging back against the pillows like a sex goddess, natural sexuality emanating from her every pore. Out of nowhere came a fierce flash of jealousy that slivered through him like a knife. Had he just taught her, or had she just taught him? Was his wife—until very recently a virgin—actually a woman with excessive experience in the foreplay department? And if she was, how could he possibly complain? After all, who was he to moralise? Why were his thoughts even running on such a theme? He was not a jealous or possessive guy. He was not one of those sad, inadequate men who questioned their partners about their previous lovers. Of course he wasn't.

'You've done that before,' Nik heard himself say.

Prudence laughed. 'No, I haven't—'

'You must've done—you've got incredible aptitude… That's OK, I'm cool with it,' Nik framed with a tense smile.

Prudence shimmied across the divide that separated them and nuzzled into connection with his lean, bronzed torso and a long, hard, hair-roughened thigh. 'I just like touching you—'

'I want you.' Sexual heat pulsing through him like a rocket charge, Nik found concentration overborne by his instinctive response to her and he flattened her to the pillows again and kissed her breathless.

The burst of passion he ignited extracted a muted gasp from her. In the space of an instant she went from languor to hunger, wildly conscious of the moist, throbbing heat at the heart of her. His wicked mouth and expert fingers teased at her swollen nipples, releasing a shower of sensual sparks inside her responsive body. A burning sense of tightness began to build low in her pelvis and it made her squirm helplessly beneath him and angle up her hips.

'You don't control the pace any more,' Nik told her thickly, surveying her with smouldering golden eyes. 'I will—'

'Partnership?'

'No…I'm an old-fashioned guy. This is the wedding night we missed out on. Just lie there and allow me to drive you out of your mind with pleasure.'

'Hmm…' Prudence ran her full mouth in a gentle foray over his strong brown throat and liked the contact and the taste of him so much that she repeated it with the tip of her tongue and the occasional nip of her teeth.

Shuddering in reaction beneath that artless onslaught of encouragement, Nik groaned. 'You're driving me wild.'

'It's my wedding night, too,' she whispered, skimming her toes down over the backs of his calves, full of leaping sexual energy.

Nik closed both hands over hers and held her captive while he gazed down at her with shimmering dark golden eyes. She looked at him with dark dilated pupils and let the tip of her tongue sneak out to wet her full lower lip.

'You're a witch.' Nik claimed her inviting lips with savage urgency, before spreading her beneath him and working his erotic passage down over her squirming body to ensure that her response to him more than equalled his to her.

When he finally traced the delicate folds at the heart of her body, she shivered violently with the hot, sweet pleasure of his caresses. The tightness deep within her became a taut, spiralling knot of desire. Her entire being, her every breath, seemed to ride on his slightest touch. Her heartbeat raced and she writhed and moaned, all control vanquished by the fierce need that made her ache. She wanted him, and she wanted and she wanted until the wanting was a frantic and ferocious craving that hurt.

Only then did he plunge into her with a single thrust of possession that jolted her with intense erotic sensation. That very intensity overwhelmed her. His hands closed to her thighs to raise her so that he could sink deeper into her tight passage. Hot, drugging pleasure engulfed her and it went on and on and on. Wild sobs of excitement escaped her. Her unbearably tense body craved release from the passionate torment of his driving rhythm. The tension built and built and then finally spilt over. With a broken cry she jerked and shivered at a peak of ecstasy that surpassed her every hope. The sweet, drowning pleasure hit her in wave after wave of joyful, quivering relief.

In the delirious aftermath she studied the strong, hard planes of his darkly handsome face and glowed inside and out with love and happiness. She held him close, smiling as he brushed his lips over her brow and returned her embrace. Such happy contentment was new to her. Wary thoughts and misgivings threatened in the back of her mind but she fought them off, determined to make the most of her bliss. For now, Nik was hers, her husband, her lover, hers alone. What did it matter if it was to prove to be just one stolen moment in time? Did she want to turn into a dreary, bitter woman who always expected the worst to happen?

'That was…astonishing, *pethi mou*,' Nik muttered raggedly, distinctly disconcerted by that truth and his own inability to explain just why sex had never been so good before. He struggled to comprehend that mystery. She was hot-blooded and so was he. She was also his wife. Was it possible that that knowledge had added some strange extra dimension? His frown line deepened, distinct unease developing, for such introspection was not a habit of his.

Prudence smiled as he crushed her to him with almost clumsy affection. He was amazingly appealing, she reflected, running loving fingers gently through his tousled black hair.

'You're so passionate.' Nik stretched lazily, enjoying the confident way she touched him. 'Yet so tranquil. We are going to have a fantastic honeymoon, Mrs Angelis.'

Prudence tensed. 'A honeymoon? You never mentioned that—'

'It's a surprise. Why do you think I've been so busy the last few weeks?' Nik continued to indolently wind a long chestnut strand of her hair round his forefinger. 'I had to clear a space for us to spend time together—'

Prudence was startled by the rush of anger that the mere mention of that word 'honeymoon' induced in her; she had never forgotten Cassia's cruel crack about that lack on her wedding day. Her pride stung as much as though he had slapped her and she shook her hair free of his hand. 'I can't possibly leave the sanctuary—'

'Of course you can. Why do you think I insisted that you take on a competent employee?'

Her temper flared at that arrogant assertion. 'You can say what you like, but I'm not leaving my animals to go off on some stupid honeymoon!'

'Oh, yes, you are,' Nik delivered. 'Had we had the same opportunity eight years ago, we would have been forced to sort out the misunderstandings and we would have had a viable marriage by the end of it. This time around we're doing everything by the book—'

'I'm sorry, but you can't rearrange my life that way. Sometimes being a responsible person entails making unselfish choices.'

Nik groaned out loud at that lofty declaration.

'And you *know* it does. Why else did you marry me eight years ago? Why else did I marry you?'

'Isn't it time we dispensed with the polite fiction that you had as little choice in that event as I had?' Nik enquired with lethal cool.

Prudence sat up, clutching the sheet to her full breasts. 'What are you trying to say?'

'You married me because you were hot for me… Let's not pretend that marrying me was any great sacrifice for you at the time!'

Prudence blinked and then lifted her lashes on shattered blue eyes. 'You are so full of yourself. That's not fair and you know it. I *didn't* have a choice. My grandfather refused to help my mother unless I married you.'

His winged ebony brows snapped together. 'Theo was to help your mother? How?' he queried. 'What are you talking about?'

'You always behave as though you gave up more than me. But I only agreed to marry you because my mother was an alcoholic in serious debt. She was drinking herself to death and rehab was her only hope—'

Thrusting back the bedding with a measured hand, Nik sprang out of bed and studied her with frowning intensity. 'Start at the beginning of the story…you said that Theo refused to help Trixie.'

'As you should know, something for nothing is not his style. He said he couldn't care less whether my mother lived or died. Unfortunately we needed his money to pay off her debts and put her into rehab. The price he demanded in return was that I marry you!'

'I didn't know…I swear I didn't know.' Nik's lean, strong face had set into hard, forbidding lines. 'Why didn't you tell me that you were under that kind of pressure?'

It was Prudence's turn to be taken aback. 'You really didn't know?'

'How could I *know* what nobody bothered to tell me?' Nik demanded fiercely.

'But you didn't ask…I just assumed you knew…I mean, I knew about your family's financial problems. But you didn't discuss that with me and, well… I wasn't in any more of a hurry to talk about the mess my mother was in,' she protested.

'I had heard that your mother had abused alcohol in the past, but by the time I met her she was almost an invalid and she was no longer drinking. I was not aware that her problems had been so recent, or that Theo didn't take full financial responsibility for her before our marriage.'

'He despised Trixie. All we ever got from my father's side of the family was the right to live at the farm. Don't get me wrong…over the years I learned to be very grateful for that security.' Prudence was marvelling that Nik could have remained in ignorance of the true facts behind their marriage for so many years without either of them appreciating the fact. Yet even as she grasped that reality, her defensiveness was replaced by a sudden surge of cringing dismay. 'Hold on a minute…you actually thought that I was so infatuated with you that I was willing to grab the first chance I got to marry you?'

Nik was stunned by the discovery that she had been as much of a victim of circumstance as he had been when they first married. '*Ne*…yes,' he admitted in Greek. 'What else could I think?'

Prudence turned white with raging humiliation. 'So, in essence, you did think that my grandfather had bought me a husband. That I was *so* desperate I would take you on any terms!'

'I need a shower, *glikia mou*.' For the first time in his life, Nik saw retreat as the most tactful response. He had believed that and, hot-headed and arrogant as he had been, it was a conviction which had filled him with considerable scorn and defiance. After all, the more cynical of his relatives had congratulated him on his good fortune on having the pulling power to attract an heiress. His pride had been battered because, like it or not, she'd had the power to rescue him and his family. Ultimately, however, he had excused and forgiven Prudence for taking him on such terms because he had always believed that she loved him. In fact, he had taken that fact absolutely for granted.

Now the picture had radically changed and Nik felt suddenly as though he had strayed into an earthquake zone. He might want to destroy Theo Demakis for treating Prudence with such callous cruelty, but he was fiercely aware that he had resorted to equally brutal tactics when Prudence asked him for a divorce. Had Prudence ever loved him? Or had it just been the crush she had said it was? After what he had just found out about their marriage eight years back, a decent guy would let her go free. His lean brown hands clenched into imprisoning fists. Well, so much for decent. What if she was in love with Leo Burleigh? She would just have to get over it, Nik decided with ferocious resolve.

Tears of frustrated fury and hurt in her eyes, Prudence curled up in a heap of throbbing mortification. How dared Nik have believed that she had been so pathetic? So mad for him that she would consent to such a marriage? Once again she was being made to appreciate how very tenuous their relationship had been when they first married. Both of them had been too proud to lower their defences and the chance to break that deadlock had never come.

At the time of their marriage, Nik's apartment had been undergoing major renovations and they had been forced to embark on married life beneath his parents' roof. They had slept in adjoining bedrooms, separated by a locked door. Surrounded by Nik's cool, distant family, she had felt more isolated and wretched than ever. Within weeks she had used the excuse of her mother's ill-health to leave Athens. She and Nik had never got to share anything. A honeymoon would certainly have made a difference.

Was she now about to let pride come between her and what might be the best chance she ever had to make something of their marriage? Shouldn't she be pleased that Nik wanted to take her away and spend time with her? Suddenly she saw how her own negative attitude might bring about what she most feared, and in dismay she scrambled out of bed. Her head swam for a split-second and she wondered if she had stood up too fast. Hearing the shower in the bathroom switch off, she pulled on Nik's discarded shirt. It smelt of his skin with a hint of the designer cologne he used. That fragrance was awesomely familiar to her and she drank it in greedily until she realised what she was doing and turned hot pink with shame over the level of her addiction to him.

'Nik…?' she said hesitantly from the threshold of the vast bathroom. Seeing it for the first time since viewing the house, she blinked in astonishment. The Victorian fittings were still in evidence but an all-singing, all-dancing array of contemporary equipment had been installed on the other side of the bathroom. 'My goodness…'

'His and hers.' Nik slicked back his wet black hair with a graceful movement of one hand. 'It's temporary until the architect comes up with a better solution.'

Prudence discovered that it was an exercise in self-denial to take her eyes from him. With a towel casually linked round his lean brown hips and crystalline drops of water caught in the black curls hazing his pectorals, Nik looked breathtakingly gorgeous.

'I've been thinking—er—reconsidering the honeymoon idea,' she mumbled. 'Possibly I was a bit, well, more than a bit ungracious. I do fuss about the sanctuary. However, with a farm manager here on the estate, I know there's no need.'

Smouldering dark golden eyes ran over her. 'None,' he confirmed. 'You look so good in my shirt I want to take it off, *thespinis mou*.'

He closed his hand over hers and drew her closer. Her mouth ran dry, her throat tightening with helpless excitement as a deep inner quiver slivered through her taut frame. She knew she should be asking him when they were leaving, but as he began to peel her out of his shirt she could not find the strength to voice the question.

Getting dressed up felt strange to Prudence: Nik had bought her a designer wardrobe before they even embarked on their honeymoon, but she had scarcely worn most of the outfits. Indeed, for almost three weeks she had lived in the barest minimum of garments. At that reflection, a bemused smile spread over her full red mouth.

Nik had brought her to Tuscany to stay in an old villa surrounded by silvery olive groves. It was a timeless place and in every sense a hideaway where the rest of the world seemed as remote as the stars. Since their arrival, Prudence had got used to being happy. As each long, lazy day melted into the next, they had become a couple. She had desperately missed that bond of friendship and affection while they had been at daggers drawn. Although they were very different personalities they held surprisingly similar opinions on many topics, but occasionally she deliberately took an opposing viewpoint just for the fun of arguing with him.

Passion simply added a very stimulating extra layer to their relationship. Even so, she was now so hooked on Nik she felt like his shadow. Every day she wakened with the same incredible sense of joyful discovery. Early-morning sunlight would filter through the shutters, casting slanting arrows of light and shadow over Nik's magnificent bronzed length, and he would stretch like an indolent tiger. Studying her with slumberous dark golden eyes, he would give her a smouldering smile and tug her back into his arms to make love to her.

Only a few weeks ago she had been afraid to trust him. Since then, however, she had learnt to be impressed by his unswerving belief that their marriage had a strong future. They spent so much time together yet they still got on like a house on fire. When they dined out in picturesque hill villages, he would walk hand-in-hand with her through the cobbled streets. That closeness, that wonderful physical warmth and acceptance, meant so much to her. Most days he had had to excuse himself for a couple of hours to deal with business matters and he would act as if her ability to amuse herself with a walk or a book or a swim was an amazing achievement.

'Maybe you're only used to helpless, dependent women,' she had contended.

'Or maybe I would like it if you acted as if you needed me occasionally.'

'Sorry…not my style.' There was a cheeky sparkle in her blue eyes and she veiled them, for she often wrapped herself round him like a vine in the middle of the night when he was fast asleep. But she reserved all such revealing demonstrations of love and need for stolen moments. After all, Nik liked to be challenged. Betraying weakness, letting him know how much she loved him, would change the balance of power forever.

Surfacing from her abstraction, Prudence reached for the turquoise sun dress she wanted to wear and put it on. It was their last day. An ache stirred in her heart and she scolded herself. Such privacy, such round-the-clock togetherness could not last forever and it would be selfish to wish that it could. The British banker Robert Donnington was an old friend of Nik's and when he had realised that Nik was in Italy he had invited them to lunch at his summer home in the Tuscan hills.

Prudence studied her reflection in the mirror. The generous swell of her bosom seemed to rise above the snugly fitting bodice and she grimaced. The dress was tighter than it had been a few weeks earlier. Was it the birth-control pills she was taking? she wondered ruefully. Her breasts had been rather sensitive of late as well. Could she be suffering from fluid retention? Or was she just refusing to face the obvious? Was she simply putting on weight as a result of the twin sins of sloth and overeating? Nik had had baklava flown in for her from Greece, and eating the honey-drenched pastries, thick with nuts, was not the road to take to being slim, Prudence conceded guiltily.

She tried on several other outfits. She was dismayed to register that virtually everything in a dressier mode was too tight for comfort at the bust. The mound of discards on the bed grew and her frustration increased because it was far too hot to be fussing over what she wore. With a sigh she put the sun dress back on, for it was comparatively loose and looked better on her than anything else had.

She walked out onto the sun-drenched terrace. 'I'm getting fat,' she told Nik morosely.

Sleek, dark and spectacular in a white shirt and beautifully cut chinos, Nik extended a lean brown hand and drew her to him. 'Don't stop eating,' he urged huskily. 'From this vantage point, I feel like I've died and gone to heaven. More can only mean sexier.'

Registering that his shamelessly intent gaze was welded to the creamy prominence of her overly abundant bosom, she shot him a look of incredulity. 'Nik!'

'I can't help it,' Nik confessed with an earthy grin of appreciation that made her heart lurch, 'I love your body. It's wonderfully voluptuous.'

That fatal word made Prudence think of a woman of generous proportions in a Rubens painting, but she said nothing. If there was anything she had learned, it was that Nik genuinely could not keep his hands off her and that had done wonders for her self-esteem. Whenever a dangerous little voice in her subconscious tried to suggest that Nik's over-active libido might explain her apparent irresistibility she refused to listen. She was determined to maintain a positive attitude. She decided that when she went home, however, she would quietly embark on a diet that would take her back down to her usual size again.

Nik curved his arms round her and pulled her back into the shelter of his big, powerful frame. Smiling, she rested back against him. The terrace had a fabulous view of the rolling hills. Dense woods of oak, cedar and black cypress gave way to lush green lines of fruitful vines and billowing fields of golden corn. The sky was a deep sapphire blue. Mellow terracotta roofs topped the ancient stone buildings that clung to a distant hilltop in the hauntingly lovely landscape.

'Close your eyes,' Nik instructed her huskily.

The sun was a warm caress on her face and another smile curved her generous mouth as he lifted her hand.

'You can look now,' he told her.

Feeling his tension, she gazed down in lively surprise at the ring that now adorned her wedding finger, and the diamond so dazzling it made her blink.

'It's an engagement ring…a proper one.'

'Oh…' Her throat convulsed, her eyes misted over. Once she had been a dreaming teenager who made a naïve romantic statement out of the prosaic presentation of a family ring and lived to learn her mistake. For that reason the significance of Nik's gift of a ring touched her to the heart, for it had been chosen especially for her and it was being given with sincerity.

'I had it engraved with our names…and the date our marriage was blessed,' Nik imparted.

'It's amazing…'

'Let it mark our new beginning.'

She gazed up at his lean, dark, angular face, as always arrestingly aware of the strong, classic planes and hollows of his fabulous bone structure. He was so incredibly handsome but even while she fought the breathless sensation he always induced she felt moved to say gently, 'You can't rewrite the past—'

'But we don't need to go there,' Nik incised in the same authoritative tone that he might have employed to teach a stubborn child a safety lesson. 'You're my wife now in every sense of the word, *thespinis mou.*'

Her tummy muscles tightened at the mere vibration of his rich, dark drawl and his words released a shocking tide of intimate memory. *In every sense*, she conceded, her mouth running dry as she acknowledged the extent of his power over her. Hot-blooded, passionate and unashamedly masculine as he was, Nik had broken down her every barrier and taught her to crave him like a drug. And in his strength was a hard core of bone-deep arrogance and obstinacy. Even as his intense charisma held her fast, she knew that he believed that he could rewrite history.

His brilliant gaze fully trained on her, Nik scored a provocative fingertip gently across her lush pink lower lip. 'And you're happy, aren't you?'

'Yes…' The sensual spell he cast made her downright dizzy with longing.

'The past…what came before doesn't count now, *thespinis mou*,' Nik drawled with immense satisfaction.

Her mobile phone buzzed and she tore her gaze from his to dig into her bag. It was Leo. 'I've got the job…I've finally got a permanent job instead of a temporary contract!'

Prudence grinned. 'Congratulations. I told you that you could do it. When will you be starting at the new school?'

'Next month. When are you coming home?'

'Tomorrow.'

'I'm going to ask Stella to help me find somewhere to live in London.'

'That's a good idea.'

'I'll be able to see a lot more of Stella and the kids when I move to the city,' Leo pronounced with satisfaction.

Prudence almost suggested that he try to find out how Stella would feel about that before he made assumptions, but decided that it would be wiser to mind her own business. Tucking her phone back in her bag, Prudence noticed that Nik's dark gaze was resting on her. 'What's wrong?'

'We're running late for lunch at the Donnington's.'

'Oh, dear, my fault…I took ages getting dressed!'

'No problem,' Nik murmured in his dark, silken drawl. 'Where's Leo's new school?'

'London.'

Nik resisted the urge to comment on how convenient London was for Oakmere Abbey. After all, he *knew* that Leo was just a friend, a rather needy character, who discussed his every move in life with Prudence. Nik had decided that Leo was a wimp, whom his wife mothered. A baby would knock Leo's current appeal stone dead, Nik thought cheerfully. Often the best solutions were the most basic and simple to execute…

CHAPTER SEVEN

A LINE OF very expensive vehicles lined the imposing approach to Robert Donnington's palatial villa outside Florence.

'I thought this was a casual lunch for just a few people,' Prudence commented in dismay, horribly conscious that her sun dress could never hope to compete with the apparel of the guests who owned such cars. But she said nothing about the latter; it was hardly Nik's fault that she had taken the word 'casual' too literally.

'That is how the invitation was presented. But Robert's daughter, Chantal, likes to party,' Nik countered with a preoccupied air.

For an inescapable moment, Nik was thinking of the reality that Theo Demakis was currently lining up the big financial guns in an effort to bring him down. Theo had no idea that the marriage he had fostered had finally blossomed. Indeed, Nik had gone to great lengths to keep the fact a secret, because he was determined to keep Theo's malign influence out of their lives. Even so, Nik was uneasily aware that he should have cut short their honeymoon and returned to London to prepare for the battle ahead. By staying on in Italy, he had left himself more exposed. Robert Donnington would back him. But the shrewd banker had already warned Nik that his sale of his multi-million-pound yacht to speed up the purchase of Oakmere Abbey had been badly timed, since it had dented his impregnable image and revealed a weak flank. Yet, given the chance to go back in time and let Oakmere go, Nik knew he would not have done anything differently; the abbey was Prudence's dream come true and, like the honeymoon, little enough recompense in his opinion for the disappointments she had endured in the past.

When Chantal Donnington came to greet them, Prudence tensed. She immediately recognised her hostess as one of Nik's exes. The willowy blonde's gushing welcome was not matched by the coolness of her green eyes, and with the excuse of taking Nik to join her father in the all-male preserve of the snooker room she divided Nik as cleanly from his wife as a surgeon.

Parked on the grandiose terrace with an alcoholic drink she didn't want, Prudence felt uncomfortably warm even in the shade. The golden heat of midday was like a blanket. She began to wonder if it was that time of the month—when she would sometimes feel under par—although it seemed like a very long time since she had suffered that particular reminder of her womanhood. She counted back the weeks and conceded that her menstrual cycle seemed to have been upset for some time. Were the birth-control pills the cause? She could not help recalling that her last period had been unusually brief. Was there a chance that the pills might not have done the trick and that she had fallen pregnant? No, that had to be wishful thinking, she scolded herself in exasperation.

Before she could dwell any longer on why she was not feeling her usual energetic and rudely healthy self, Chantal Donnington came over and trilled, 'Let me introduce you to a couple of guests who are just dying to meet you…'

Prudence's eyes widened when she saw a leggy dark-haired beauty in an outrageously short skirt approaching her. The brunette was accompanied by a spiky-haired blonde dressed in the sort of clinging white dress that only a very thin woman could aspire to wearing. Unless she was very much mistaken, and Prudence did not think her memory was at fault, she was about to meet another two of Nik's former lovers. The feminine antagonism in the air made the skin prickle at the nape of her neck.

'I'm Jenna Marsden,' the brunette announced tautly.

'Zoe Amberley,' the blonde supplied with a challenging smile. 'You may not be aware of the fact but we all have something in common.'

'Nik…' Prudence saw no point in pretending ignorance.

'Nik Angelis is an extraordinary guy.' Zoe's husky voice made a suggestive meal of the statement and Prudence's tension increased. 'Quite unforgettable.'

'Yes, he certainly lives up to his legendary reputation.' Chantal rested spiteful green eyes on Prudence.

Although colour had blossomed over her cheekbones, Prudence just smiled as though she had the skin of a rhinoceros. 'Doesn't he just?'

'When Chantal mentioned that Nik's wife would be here today, Zoe and I agreed that we just *had* to meet you as well,' Jenna declared in a defensive rush that suggested that she was uncomfortable with the animosity in the air. 'What's it like being married to him?'

'Fabulous.' Prudence was striving not to feel cowed by the fact that she had three women a foot taller than she was towering over her. Actually, it was their sheer physical beauty rather than their height that intimidated her. Every comparison she had most feared was now in front of her in full daylight and living flesh: women with perfect faces and sleek, stunning bodies without flaw. No ordinary woman could bear such a cruel contrast. How could Nik *not* feel that his wife was less than what he deserved? Yet had Nik not made his choice of his own free will? And Nik, she reminded herself doggedly, was no fool and no sacrificial lamb either.

'I would not live with Nik's womanising,' Zoe pronounced in a pitying tone.

'I would have far too much pride,' Chantal affirmed.

Prudence wore an expression of polite surprise because Nik had never, to her knowledge, offered any of his mistresses his exclusive attention. Or even pretended to do so.

'Any other woman would have divorced him long ago,' Zoe sneered.

Prudence could only think of how hard Nik had fought to stay married to her and a secretive little smile curved her full mouth in answer.

When Nik emerged from the villa and saw the three women surrounding Prudence, he went rigid. It could be no coincidence that another two of his exes should be present at a social engagement in Italy. He was outraged that Prudence should have become a target for his sins. Dark fury and concern flashing through his big, powerful frame, his lean, bronzed face hard, he strode across the terrace.

'Ladies…Zoe, Jenna,' Nik acknowledged, cool as ice, curving a protective arm to Prudence's tense spine. 'You must excuse us…'

Disconcerted by his sudden appearance, Chantal loosed a rather forced laugh. 'We were just curious, Nik. My goodness, you don't need to come rushing to your wife's rescue. All we really want to know is…what makes Prudence so very special?'

A razor-edged smile slashed Nik's hard mouth. 'She never forgets that she's a lady.'

As their companions absorbed that smooth, cutting

counter-attack with varying degrees of discomfiture, Nik swept Prudence off to introduce her to Robert Donnington and soon afterwards lunch was served. At the table she and Nik were seated separately.

Jenna settled down into the chair next to Prudence. 'It took me so long to get over Nik,' she confided plaintively. 'I fell into a rebound romance after him and that went wrong, too.'

'You're so lovely, you're sure to meet someone else,' Prudence told her gently.

'But not someone like Nik,' the exquisite brunette lamented.

'You should concentrate on what annoyed you most about him,' Prudence advised.

The stress of deep thought was clearly marked on Jenna's lovely face. 'He never phoned…he wouldn't go to parties, business always came first,' she recited obediently.

With charged disbelief, Nik looked down the table half an hour later and saw his wife and Jenna Marsden laughing together as though they were the warmest of old friends. Glancing up, Prudence met Nik's burnished golden appraisal and ready colour warmed her complexion. His attention lingered on her and a wicked little *frisson* of heat and awareness awakened in her pelvis. While Jenna continued to give her chapter and verse on her most recent romantic disappointment, Prudence found her gaze continually stealing back to Nik's bold dark profile. Catching her watching him again, he flashed her a look and a smile which sizzled with a raw, erotic understanding that mesmerised her and set her treacherous body on fire. Nik could convey desire and invitation with a single flash of his stunning eyes.

It became an effort for Prudence to concentrate on what her companion was telling her. Mortified by the swollen sensitivity of her nipples, Prudence stopped looking in Nik's direction altogether but it was a punishment to practise such self-denial. She wanted him. He had made her shameless. He had taught her a desire she could not quench. Love and longing, she acknowledged, were destroying her self-control.

Fresh drinks were being served when Nik appeared by her side without warning. Without giving her the chance to ask what was happening, he assisted her out of her seat with cool assurance.

'I've explained that the jet is on standby and that we have to leave now,' Nik spelt out quietly.

Prudence gathered that some business crisis was demanding that they leave Italy a day sooner than planned. Disappointment assailed her, for she had cherished every hour of their time at the villa. To have Nik all to herself for so long had been a joy and to lament the loss of a single day was childish and ungrateful, she told herself sharply. As they left the terrace she was conscious of Chantal and Zoe watching Nik with a blatant hunger that neither could hide. It shook her to see such naked sexual longing.

But was she any stronger or wiser where Nik was concerned? Did she look at him the same way? Sudden doubt and fear gripped Prudence. Barely three weeks ago, she had seen Nik as the enemy and she had been full of fighting fervour with all her defences in place. But Nik had triumphed over her fears and her insecurities by the most simple and yet subtle moves. He had treated her to a glorious honeymoon in Italy, introduced her to a passion that was indecently absorbing and had awarded her the heady effect of his entire attention. Was it any wonder that he currently had her eating out of his hand like a pet dove? And was she really planning to let that humiliating state of affairs continue?

He brought the Ferrari to a halt a couple of miles down the road. 'Come here...' he urged with husky impatience.

Dragged from the depths of her disturbing reflections, Prudence blinked. 'Sorry? What's wrong?'

'Wrong?' Gold fire leaping in his spectacular eyes, Nik released her seat belt and tugged her forward, saying with hungry appreciation, 'Nothing's wrong. A wife who can arouse me in a public place just by looking at me is a magnificent gift, not a problem. I got us out of there before I embarrassed you…'

Prudence belatedly appreciated what had prompted their speedy departure from the Donnington's: *lust*. She recalled the manner in which she had watched him. Wide-eyed with disconcertion, she blushed to the roots of her hair. 'You mean, we're not really racing back to the villa to pack and head for the airport?'

'We will be racing—only not to the airport. But first let me have a taste of you, *pethi mou*.' Nik bent his arrogant dark head. He toyed with the luscious fullness of her lower lip, gently nipping and grazing the tender skin and provoking helpless whimpers of eager response from her. Tilting her head back, she offered him her whole mouth as a playground and he set every pulse in her quivering body aflame with the measured thrust of his tongue.

His strong bone structure taut beneath his bronzed skin, he set her back from him and did up her seat belt again with a lot less cool than he had employed undoing it. Scorching golden eyes melded to hers in a stormy collision. 'I'm so hot for you I'm in pain but we can't make love here,' he pointed out raggedly, directing the powerful car back onto the road.

'I'm not used to you behaving like this,' she admitted breathlessly but she was trying so hard not to smile from ear to ear, for she had a wicked sense of achievement. He had just taught her how susceptible he could be and she was a fast learner. She knew that some day she would use that lesson to her advantage.

'I'm not used to it either.' Nik vented a rough laugh. 'Perhaps it's partly fired by admiration. Most women would have thrown a scene over being confronted by Chantal and co....'

Prudence winced. 'What would have been the point?'

'You handled it in a very stylish way. When I saw you talking to Jenna, though, I did wonder what you were talking about,' he admitted.

His expectant silence stretched. Smiling inside herself, Prudence said nothing. Let him wonder what had been discussed! She eyed her dazzling diamond ring with new complacency. She was amazed that she had been fretting about the state of their relationship only minutes earlier. There she had been, ready to get all worked up when she had nothing to worry about!

When the silence ticked on unbroken, Nik responded to the challenge. 'There will be no other women in my life now that I have you.'

Prudence felt as if the sun had just risen inside her. These were the promise, the commitment, the words she had needed to hear, but would never have asked him to give her. 'That's good. Particularly because I would be very unladylike and very unforgiving in the way I handled infidelity,' she told him softly.

Disconcerted though he was by that immediate warning, Nik almost laughed in appreciation of her timing. She was so different from every other woman he had ever known. She had no fear of him and she stood up to him. But she was no drama queen. Had it never dawned on Theo Demakis that his granddaughter was as clever as he was? It hadn't dawned on her stupid husband, Nik acknowledged ruefully, wondering what else he still had to discover about his wife.

At the villa, Nik lifted Prudence out of the car and right up into his arms to kiss her with raw hunger and need. She melted into his lean, hard body, exulting in his strength and burying her fingers in his luxuriant black hair.

'I want you so bad, *thespinis mou*,' he growled against her swollen mouth, moving across the threshold of their room as he backed her towards the bed.

He angled her back against him and dealt summarily with the straps of her dress and the cups of her bra, groaning with satisfaction when her luscious breasts spilled free into his appreciative hold. Her legs trembled. She was hot and shivering and weak all at once. He captured the straining pink peaks between his fingers and she gasped out loud. The sensation of tightness in her pelvis increased to an almost unbearable degree.

'Nik…please,' she moaned, utterly helpless in the grip of that pulse beat of desire.

'So glad you're suffering, too…' Nik let his teeth graze her soft, creamy shoulder while he wrenched her out of the dress with such a lack of finesse that the fabric tore. He ran his tongue down her spine, curved caressing hands to shape the sensual swell of her bottom and dropped to his knees to slowly, carefully, sexily remove her panties.

'Oh…' Her teeth chattered together in reaction as he found the most sensitive spot on her entire body with his mouth. She shut her eyes tight, wild pleasure and erotic shock at that sudden intimacy travelling through her shivering length in waves. Hot liquid sensation pulsed through her for long, timeless moments. She was out of control and loving it.

He tumbled her back on the bed. Scorching golden eyes raked her with sensual ferocity. 'I can't wait…'

'Take your shirt off…'

He hauled it off with such violence that buttons went flying.

Prudence feasted her eyes on him, wondered if she could

wait until he got the rest of his clothes off and decided that she couldn't. She opened her arms, arched her spine and shifted her hips in silent invitation.

His burning gaze flared with white-hot desire. 'You tease…' he ground out helplessly, coming down to her with flattering impatience, all fire, hunger and aggressive masculine energy.

He plunged into her tender flesh with a sweet force that made her cry out. Nothing had ever been as wild as the passion they generated in that fiery fusion. Her excitement was incredibly intense. He drove her to a shattering peak of passion and the intolerable pleasure took her by storm. The power of the experience left her dazed and full of warmth and emotion.

Nik lifted his damp, dark head, smouldering eyes raking her flushed face. His charismatic smile curved his mobile mouth and he claimed her reddened lips in a tender kiss. 'You amazing woman…'

She wanted to tell him that she loved him but bit back the revealing words just in time. Even so she felt so happy she wanted to cry and she buried her head in his shoulder, breathing in the scent of his damp, tawny skin with blissful satisfaction. She felt as if he was hers now, wholly, entirely, absolutely hers.

'I wonder if we made a baby this time,' Nik murmured huskily.

Consternation tensed Prudence's small frame. A spasm of pure, naked guilt travelled through her, because she had made no attempt to tell him that she was taking precautions against pregnancy. Of course, she had noticed that he had made no attempt to guard against that risk. She had, she was ashamed to admit, felt a tad superior in her knowledge that she was in full, if secret, control of her own fertility. But that had been right back at the beginning when she didn't trust him and believed she wanted a divorce. Everything had changed since then. She knew that this was the moment when she should speak up, but it seemed to her that such a confession would make things very complicated and might even damage the new bonds they had formed.

'You're very quiet.' Nik rested back on his elbow, watching her from below sinfully long black eyelashes, his lean, bronzed features achingly handsome. 'I know how much you want a child.'

Prudence squirmed like a butterfly on a pin, torn by the knowledge of her deception. 'Yes—er—well, but—'

'I got used to the idea of having a family very fast. I like it,' Nik confided, pure devilment gleaming in his clear gaze as he let a seemingly idle hand stray from her waist down to her thigh and linger there. 'I like working on the project of making you a mother. I intend to devote an enormous amount of time and effort to that challenge…any objections?'

'None…' Even in the grip of shame over her craven lack of candour, Prudence could not resist that look and even less could she resist his touch. She would just stop taking the pills and he would never know, she thought weakly, quivering with anticipation and excitement as he shifted fluidly closer.

Prudence assumed lack of sleep was to blame for her low appetite at breakfast the next day. She also felt ever so slightly nauseous. Mid-morning they flew back to London. Prudence was so eager to see how her rescue animals had fared during her absence that she changed into practical clothes on the flight and asked to be delivered straight to the stable yard.

Five minutes later, the limo pulled up outside the abbey. As Nik climbed out he kicked over the handbag that Prudence had left lying on the floor. The soft caramel leather holdall he had bought her in Florence tipped out its contents onto the gravel of the driveway. His gaze arrowed in on the foil-packed strip that lay half-in, half-out of the bag. Bending down, he lifted it and fell very still.

CHAPTER EIGHT

WITH DOTTIE'S HELP, Prudence placed baskets for her elderly dogs, Sooty and Minnie, into a cosy back hall and settled them there, since the cook had made it clear that he was no fan of four-legged animals in the kitchen quarters.

The older woman was defensive on Prudence's behalf. 'Oakmere is your home. You should just tell that fancy chef that he has to put up with the dogs!'

'The kitchen's his territory now and thank goodness that it is. I hate cooking,' Prudence reminded her equably. 'Not everyone approves of animals indoors.'

Prudence had never lived without at least a couple of dogs at her heels. She was keenly aware, however, that Nik had grown up without pets and was not accustomed to sharing accommodation with them. Dottie took her leave. Prudence was eager to explore the house and see how the renovations were coming on but it was getting late. Still muddy and more than a little bedraggled from the evening routine of watering and feeding, she hurried upstairs to shower and change before dinner. She also felt incredibly tired and thought that perhaps it was time she had a medical check-up. After all, she reminded herself, her menstrual cycle still seemed to be out of kilter and that was unusual.

Twenty minutes later Prudence emerged from the bathroom, wrapped in a towel and with her wet hair combed back from her brow. Nik was stationed by the tall bedroom windows. Her eyes lit up and eager words about how well the sanctuary had fared during her absence were bubbling on her lips. But when Nik swung round, she saw the grim darkness of his gaze and the forbidding cast of his strong, dark features and her tummy flipped in alarm.

'What's up? What's happened?' she questioned.

In answer, Nik tossed the packet of pills at her feet.

Prudence gulped and folded her lips, her guilt and dismay unconcealed. 'Oh, dear…'

'Is that all you've got to say to me?' Nik countered grittily.

Prudence floundered and sidestepped that direct question. 'The packet was in my handbag…how did you get hold of it?'

'I tripped over your bag in the limo and it fell out.'

Her colour high, Prudence stopped trying to evade the confrontation. She drew in a steadying breath. 'I had already decided to stop taking them—'

'And when did you take that momentous decision?'

Prudence reddened because she knew that her answer would not impress him. 'Last night…'

His thunderous aspect remained undiminished. 'When did you organise contraception?'

She told him.

'So, you've been lying to me from the minute that we began living together as husband and wife.'

Prudence squirmed but sought to defend herself. 'That's a very emotive way of putting it—'

His dark gaze flashed gold and his dark, deep voice was dangerously quiet. 'And how would you suggest I put it?'

'As it *was*…rather than how it is now—'

'That's not relevant—'

'It is. I made that decision in the past—'

'What's at stake here is trust,' Nik delineated.

'Yes, but the circumstances—'

'Don't count.' His lean, bronzed face was unyielding. 'You should have told me you were using birth control. That was a matter for us both to discuss. But then that isn't what this is about, is it? You preferred to go behind my back and deceive me.'

Prudence could feel the outrage he was containing. It was there in the rigidity with which he was holding his lithe, powerful body, in the burnished gold in his eyes and the prominence of his hard, classic cheekbones. She wanted to scream with frustration and regret. Everything had been so wonderful, so perfect, and the future so promising. He need never have known that she was taking those wretched pills. Why on earth hadn't she immediately disposed of the evidence?

In the midst of that train of thought, she was shocked by other, sneaky ideas travelling through her head. Hadn't she always believed in complete honesty? What had happened to that? Nik had come back into her life and Nik was more important to her than anything else. That was why she had fallen off the straight and narrow path so fast her head was still spinning. She had wanted to preserve their relationship, not tear it apart.

'In spite of all the time we were together in Italy, you said not a word about the fact that you were using contraception,' Nik ground out in the rushing silence.

'I didn't think about it, not properly,' Prudence said defensively. 'I've just been so busy being happy with you—'

'Really…happy?' Nik framed in his slick, dark drawl that could be so incredibly sardonic in tone. 'It was a great act. You wanted a baby, but there was no damned way you were about to risk that baby being mine!'

'That's not true and I wasn't acting—'

'A couple of months ago, you were willing to go to a sperm bank and choose a stranger to father your child…but I wasn't good enough– '

'That's ridiculous,' she gasped. 'I just wasn't ready to talk about this with you—'

'You weren't going to tell me at all. Do you think I don't realise that?'

Prudence was so tense that her spine was hurting. 'You're not being fair, Nik—'

'How fair were you?' Nik countered in a wrathful undertone, his impassive façade starting to crack to reveal his cold, seething anger. 'How fair were you being when you let me believe that we were trying to start a family? I wanted that child for your sake. I could have waited. I didn't want a child until I realised that that was your biggest dream. Is this how you repay me for trying to give you what I thought you wanted? With lies and deception?'

And that was the precise moment that Prudence truly grasped how much damage she had done to their marriage and she was horrified. The halter she had had on her own emotions snapped beneath that pressure. 'What choice did you give me at the beginning? I had no idea what to expect from you,' she protested. 'You forced me to make our marriage real and I had to protect myself as best I could. I had to think ahead—'

'*Theos mou*…was everything we shared a complete con?' Nik launched at her rawly. 'Were you just pretending to be happy as well?'

Her sense of panic increased, for she felt as though she was being boxed into an ever tighter corner. 'No, of course not. But I didn't know how things were going to turn out between us before we went to Italy and that's why I started taking birth-control pills. I couldn't take the risk of falling pregnant. If I'd had a baby with you, it would have given you even more of a hold over me.'

'You could have told me that upfront—'

'I didn't think about it at the beginning and, by the time I did, it seemed too awkward and controversial—'

His lean, powerful face had hardened. 'Maybe it gave you a kick to put one over on me.'

Prudence was too worked up to pick and choose her words. 'Yes, once or twice it did…'

Beneath his bronzed skin, Nik lost colour at that unexpected admission. He rested raw dark eyes on her, aggression leaping from every taut inch of his magnificent body. 'You are not the woman I thought you were—'

Prudence felt her tummy flip as if she was teetering on the edge of a dangerous chasm. 'Perhaps I shouldn't have admitted that and I'm certainly not proud of it but I have feelings, too. I was very angry with you at the start, but I was scared as well—'

'Scared?' Nik interrupted wrathfully. 'You have never in your entire life had cause to be scared of me!'

'How about when you told me my animals could go hang if I didn't agree to give our marriage a trial?'

Nik shrugged an elegant shoulder and spread expressive lean brown hands in denial of that reminder. 'It was just an empty threat, part of the negotiations. I knew right from the start that you would give in. Believe me, I would never have allowed any harm whatsoever to come to your animals.'

'I'd like to say that I believe you, but I can't. You're not the world's most compassionate person, Nik. Once I wouldn't accept that side of you. I idealised you and it was very foolish of me,' Prudence confided unhappily. 'After all, your reputation always said you were a bastard…and when I crossed you, I discovered that you were much more callous than I had ever wanted to appreciate.'

In receipt of that ringing indictment of his character, Nik had gone very still. He was shocked; he had enjoyed her romantic view of him as almost perfect. A very faint darkening of colour demarcated the slashing line of his fabulous cheekbones and then it faded, leaving him unusually pale. 'That's not how I am—'

'It's the only way you know how to be. You're tough and incredibly domineering, Nik. You just lay down the law, you demand, you expect—'

Nik rested brilliant dark eyes of reproach on her. 'That is not how I behaved in Italy. That is not how I treat you, *thespinis mou.*'

The hostility in the air and the taste of her own fear for the future scared Prudence but she refused to back down. 'I agree…but that still doesn't change how this marriage started out last month. Why are you trying to ignore the facts? You coerced me into doing what I didn't want to do…just as my grandfather once did…and there was no way I was going to sit back and take that again!'

'That's not an excuse for taking contraceptive pills to ensure that you didn't have my baby,' Nik condemned roughly, his Greek accent raking round every syllable of that abrasive comeback.

'Everything's changed since I took that decision.'

'But my sins have come back to haunt me. Some would say that is very appropriate and deserved,' Nik said quietly.

'I wouldn't…'

But Nik was no longer focusing on her. His striking gaze seemed to be looking inward and the sombre cast of his features struck a chill into her bones.

'Don't be like this—'

Nik rested brooding dark eyes on her. 'How else do you expect me to be?'

Prudence moved towards him and made a tiny placatory gesture with one hand, before hurriedly squeezing her fingers together and letting her hand drop back to her side. In such a mood he would reject her and all bravery deserted her in the face of that prospect. 'Don't think that I don't appreciate that you've had to be tough to survive,' she told him awkwardly. 'Your whole family depend on you and I know that you had to be a hard-hitter to break away from my grandfather and still stay in business.'

Nik bit out a harsh laugh, for she had not the slightest idea that once again he was fighting to stand firm against the might of Demakis International. But that was how it should be in his opinion: it was his duty to protect her from such worries. He cherished the memory of her happiness in Tuscany. 'Is this my wife making excuses for me for being a bastard? Don't waste your time. I'm not ashamed of what I am.'

Prudence could feel the hostile distance in him and that was when she realised how much damage had been done to their marriage. He was Greek and he was very proud. At the end of the day, family meant everything. She knew that the belief that she did not want his child must have cut deep. 'I didn't want to tell you about the pills, because I knew they would create a stupid misunderstanding.'

Nik shrugged a broad shoulder with magnificent cool. 'What's to misunderstand? As I said, I didn't want a child until I made the error of assuming that you were desperate for one. Keep taking the pills with my blessing,' he urged. 'Look, I have to go into the office. A lot has been happening on the business front while we were sunning ourselves in Italy.'

Dismay and disappointment assailed Prudence. Just when she had given him her trust, just when she was ready to openly admit to him how very much she wanted to have a child with him, Nik had withdrawn the possibility and shut the door in her face. Even worse, his use of that word 'desperate' in relation to her feelings about babies sealed her lips on any protest. She did not want to figure as desperate in Nik's eyes, not when he made it so plain that he had only ever been willing to consider fatherhood for her benefit.

'Is that really how you feel?' Prudence prompted tightly, with tears burning the backs of her eyes and her throat aching.

Nik opened the door. 'How else would I feel?'

In considerably less demand than a sperm bank, he thought to himself in answer to that question when he was safely on the other side of the door. He wanted to punch a hole in the wall. He needed to vent the explosive emotions attacking his usually clear thinking processes. That violent urge shook his view of himself, but Prudence had deceived him and he had fallen for it hook, line and sinker. His destructive thoughts raged on: how did he know that she had *ever* planned to use a sperm bank to have a child? Had he given her the divorce she had so badly wanted, would he then have discovered that Leo Burleigh was destined to become the father of her children? A sperm bank? Prudence, who was so conventional? Had that ever been a credible tale?

Once again, it seemed, he had underestimated his wife. She had seen through the façade and realised that he was a callous bastard. Nik raked long brown fingers viciously through his black hair and then studied his hand with a frown, for it had developed a slight tremor. What was the matter with him? At a time when he was fighting for survival in business he needed all his wits and his strength. Never had he been unequal to a challenge, he reminded himself fiercely. At best he had been on trial during their honeymoon. At worst Prudence was planning to walk out on him for another man. Why else would a woman who had been so keen to have a baby now guard so carefully against the possibility?

By the time Prudence got dressed and went off in pursuit of Nik, it was too late: he had gone. Panic threatened to take her over. She lifted the phone to call him and then hesitated. Wouldn't it be wiser to wait until he came home? She could then talk to him with calm and sense. At present, she acknowledged, she felt neither calm nor sensible. In fact, she felt frantic and tearful and furious and hurt and terrified. Nik had been honest: he didn't want a baby. She thought it was wonderful that he could admit that while censuring her for practising birth control. But the reflection was of little consolation to her. What really mattered to her was that she had hurt his pride and disappointed him and she blamed herself bitterly for not being more honest with him in Italy.

The evening passed slowly, enlivened only by a call from Leo, who asked her to view a couple of properties with him later in the week. It was after midnight when Nik finally phoned to say that he would be working right into the early hours and staying at the apartment. Listening to the low voices and the bustle she could hear in the background, Prudence swallowed her disappointment and tried to act as if nothing was wrong. Maybe it was a good idea to let the dust settle, she told herself unhappily.

Nik was away for two days, and on the third evening, when he did return to Oakmere, it was Prudence who was absent from home and hearth. Nik went all over the habitable rooms, looking for a note. Then he went down to the stable yard and checked the sheds and the fields but there was no sign of his wife anywhere. When there was no other choice he rang her on her mobile phone.

'Where are you?' Nik enquired a shade tersely when she answered.

'I'm viewing an apartment in London with Leo…'

Nik breathed in very deep and slow.

'Are you still working?'

'No. I came home to spend time with you.'

'And I'm out…what a shame,' Prudence lamented with all the seeming regret that any man could wish to hear. 'I didn't think you'd be back tonight.'

Nik found that confession far from comforting. What if handsome, attentive Leo wasn't just a friend? How could he know for sure? Leo did nothing without consulting Prudence first. He rang Prudence continually and Prudence was attached to him. In comparison, Nik was conscious that he himself was at a severe disadvantage. He had coerced Prudence into living with him. She didn't love him. Taking into account what she had said about his character, his wife didn't like him very much either, he reflected heavily. But she still couldn't keep her hands off him. Sexually he was very much in demand. Or had that been an act, too? A matter of good, clean fun? Prudence was a deeply sensual woman. And a deeply sensual woman, who had waited so long to explore that side of her nature, might well want to experiment…

'Nik?' Prudence pressed in the humming silence. 'Look, I have to go. I'll see you later.'

It was very much later by the time that Prudence finally walked wearily through the ancient front door of the abbey. All she wanted to do was lie down and sleep for a month. Her desire to hurry home had been frustrated at every turn. Nik greeted her at the foot of the stairs. The minute she saw him butterflies flew loose in her tummy. He looked so achingly handsome that she couldn't drag her eyes from his lean, dark face.

'Where have you been?' Nik demanded. 'I tried to ring you again. You didn't answer your phone.'

'It's dead. I forgot to charge it,' she sighed. 'You wouldn't believe the trouble I've had getting home—'

'Try me,' Nik invited.

'Leo spent ages talking to the vendor at the property we viewed. When I got back to my car it had a flat tyre... Leo changed it but he had a dreadful time with the wheel nuts.' Prudence threaded her hair off her damp brow with limp fingers and wished she could just sit down and slump.

'Wheel nuts,' Nik repeated with glittering dark golden eyes. 'Is that the best you can do for an excuse?'

Blinking in bewilderment, she paused on her passage up the massive staircase. 'I beg your pardon?'

'It's after midnight—'

'I'm not Cinderella—'

'And I'm not stupid. You've been with another man for hours on end.'

'Another man?' Prudence frowned, not immediately able to identify Leo as falling within that category.

'You don't answer your phone...you've been gone all evening. Naturally I'm suspicious.'

When Prudence realised what Nik was driving at she could not hide her astonishment. 'Suspicious of Leo and me? But he's madly in love with Stella and has been for years—'

'Isn't it strange that you never mentioned a Stella before?'

His persistence disconcerted her. The charged tension etched in his bronzed features was very real. Only then did she recall her silence when he had questioned her friendship with Leo after that misleading photo had appeared in the newspaper. She felt horribly guilty because she had made no attempt to settle his suspicions then and there. In fact she had actually quite enjoyed the idea that he was no longer so sure that her affections were firmly centred on him.

'Leo and I are mates and that's all. I should have made that clear from the start. The trouble is…I quite liked you being a bit jealous,' Prudence confided shamefacedly, wincing at an odd little shooting pain low in her tummy.

'I don't do jealous,' Nik asserted between gritted white teeth.

Fighting off a sick wave of dizziness, Prudence acknowledged that she really wasn't feeling very well and she gripped the balustrade hard. Her complexion was paper white.

'*Theos mou*…What's wrong?' Nik exclaimed.

Prudence swayed as her knees began to buckle and the darkness folded in. Nik threw himself forward and caught her in his arms as she fainted.

Prudence swam back to consciousness. She was lying on a sofa in the drawing room. 'What happened?'

Nik was bending over her. His brilliant, beautiful dark eyes were full of concern. 'You passed out and almost fell down the stairs. I think you need to see a doctor—'

'Don't be daft. There's nothing the matter with me. I just think I overdid things today. I haven't had anything to eat and I'm tired,' she muttered ruefully.

'Leo really looks after you, *pethi mou*,' Nik derided.

'A woman doesn't need a man to look after her.'

'It's a pleasure for me to look after you…to see that you eat and rest and have no worries,' Nik responded without hesitation. 'I *like* doing it.'

It was true and he did it so well. She remembered his solicitous behaviour in Tuscany. It had encompassed everything from ensuring she didn't sit too long in the sun to letting her lie in bed longer than he did in the morning. They had dined at her favourite restaurants, visited the places she most wanted to see. He had spoilt her rotten and made her feel as precious as solid gold. Without thinking about it, she reached for his hand and pushed her cheek into his palm in a helpless gesture of affection.

The tension etched in his lean, hard features eased. Long brown fingers stroked her face. 'I still want a doctor to check you out tomorrow. You look too fragile.'

With his help she got into bed. He brought her an omelette which he swore he had cooked himself and while she ate he invited her to tell him about Leo and Stella. He laughed a couple of times. He said Leo was mucking about and acting like a wimp. Arguing with that macho judgement, Prudence began to relax and feel happy again. She had missed Nik so much. The giant hole in her life had felt unendurable. So what if he didn't want children? she asked herself wryly. She could learn to live with that. Nothing was perfect. At some time in the future he might change his mind. If she had him, if she had the guy she loved, shouldn't that be enough for her?

'I should've told you about the pills,' she whispered in drowsy apology.

'No…you were right. I let myself forget how our marriage started out.' Dark golden eyes sombre, Nik watched her slide into sleep. Earlier that day he had put Oakmere Abbey in her name so that whatever happened she and the sanctuary would be secure. The estate would be self-sufficient. If he wasn't careful he would lose her as well as everything else. Somehow, some way, he had to address the image problem, he reflected grimly, fighting off his exhaustion. Subscribing to charity and pioneering business-enterprise awards for the young weren't enough to impress Prudence. He had to do something compassionate in the animal line.

In the early hours, Prudence woke up and smiled sleepily at the familiar feel of Nik's lean, hot, powerful body against hers. She lifted her lashes to study him. He was wide awake and watching her, too, golden eyes steady. He looked so serious and she wondered why, but only briefly, for the blue-black stubble shadowing his classic chiselled features only added to his smouldering sex appeal. Shifting closer, she gave an encouraging little wriggle. Surprised by his failure to take immediate advantage, she smoothed a provocative hand down over his hard, bronzed torso. He caught her fingers in his. 'You were ill last night…we shouldn't—'

'Refusal will offend. You said it was your pleasure to look after me,' Prudence reminded him with dancing eyes.

An appreciative grin slashed his handsome mouth. 'It is…a very great pleasure, *thespinis mou*,' he asserted, tugging her up against him with easy strength and taking her mouth with passionate fervour.

A couple of hours later she hurried downstairs to join Nik for breakfast. She was crossing the hall when without the slightest warning a spasm of sharp pain gripped her pelvis and doubled her up. 'Nik!' she gasped in shock and fear.

He took her to the nearest hospital. They were both totally stunned when a pregnancy test was carried out and came up with a positive result. Before Prudence could even deal with the knowledge that she was almost two months pregnant, she learned that she was losing her baby. Ashen below his bronzed skin, Nik listened with hollow, dark eyes when the gynaecologist opined that the very lack of symptoms that might have initially warned Prudence of her condition might well have indicated an unstable pregnancy. No, he assured her kindly, he did not think that she could have done anything to change what was happening. After that there was nothing to do but let nature take its course.

When it was all over she lay in her private room, staring sightlessly at the wall. She must have fallen pregnant the very first time she slept with Nik. Her most cherished dream had come true with the man she loved, but she had not had the chance to enjoy the fact even briefly.

'I wish we'd known,' Nik breathed thickly, gripping her

hand in his. 'It feels so wrong that we didn't know until it was too late.'

'No,' she agreed numbly, staring at the wall at the foot of the bed.

'I am to blame for this situation. We made love and I chose not to protect you—'

'I said I wanted a child,' she said dully, not understanding how he was to blame. She had conceived and would have been overjoyed had she still been pregnant. But now she had miscarried and all such talk only reminded her of her loss and her disappointment.

Nik closed both hands round her limp fingers and expelled his breath in a ragged hiss. 'I'm so sorry…you will probably never understand how much.'

He had stayed with her throughout. He had been strong for her, supportive, everything a husband should be. But only a few days back he had admitted that he didn't really want a baby with her. Of course, had he realised that there was the slightest risk that she might be pregnant he would never have admitted that. But he had admitted it and she could not forget his candour. And, naturally, he could not forget it on such a day either. After all, Prudence conceded wretchedly, he was a very decent guy.

'I let my pride come between us…' Nik bit out in a driven undertone.

That was a startling enough announcement to make Prudence turn her head on the pillow to look directly at him. 'How?'

Nik studied her with bleak, dark eyes. 'I wanted you to have my child. But I wouldn't admit that when the sentiment wasn't returned.'

Her throat thickened. She turned her head away again and squeezed her eyes tight shut on the tears threatening to well up and overflow. He was trying to comfort her by demonstrating his sympathy and understanding of her feelings. He was really, really good at that, she acknowledged inwardly. He always knew exactly what to say. But she did not want him telling her lies out of pity or out of guilt. Why should he feel guilty because he had said he didn't want a baby? Lots of guys of Nik's age and lifestyle would feel exactly the same.

'I think I want to sleep,' she murmured flatly.

'Go ahead…I won't disturb you.'

The silence stretched.

'I'd like to be on my own,' she muttered tightly.

'But I don't think you should be, *pethi mou.*'

'Just go home,' she told him stonily. 'Don't you have any work to do?'

The silence thundered. The door closed. She flipped over and focused on the chair he had vacated. She had wanted him to go but, just as swiftly and unreasonably, she wanted him back. The thickness in her throat became great gulping sobs and she rolled back and buried her face in the pillow.

Three days later, Nik picked her up and took her back to Oakmere. She changed the subject whenever he tried to talk about the miscarriage…

It was six weeks since Prudence had returned from hospital. She could hear a phone ringing in the abbey's cavernous entrance hall. The housekeeper answered it before she could reach it and brought the phone to her.

'Am I speaking to Prudence Angelis?' an accented male voice enquired heavily. 'The granddaughter of Theo Demakis?'

She frowned. 'Yes…why?'

It was her grandfather's lawyer, Gregoly Lelas. He was calling to inform her that the older man had died very suddenly that morning from a massive heart attack. Shock engulfed Prudence in a sickening tide. She had always cherished the secret hope that Theo Demakis would come to regret his treatment of her and wish to get to know her as a member of his family. But now it was too late, forever too late because he was gone.

As her pale profile pinched tight, Nik strode into the room. 'What has happened?'

'My grandfather's dead,' she mumbled sickly.

CHAPTER NINE

'HOW DO YOU feel?' Nik settled Prudence into a seat on his private jet with as much care as he would have utilised had she been an invalid.

'I'm perfectly fine.' Her even white teeth clenched on that declaration. She was convinced that if he asked her one more time how she was, she would scream! Such prolonged, exaggerated solicitude struck her as quite unnecessary. She was not suffering any physical discomfort or weakness now. Ironically she felt healthy as a horse.

When they were airborne, Prudence studied a wildlife magazine and struggled to seem unconscious of Nik's steady regard.

'You're not speaking to me…' Nik murmured.

'Of course I'm speaking to you. I'm not a child, for goodness' sake!'

'I don't know you like this. It's like you're surrounded by barbed wire.'

'We are on our way to a funeral. Excuse me for not feeling chatty,' Prudence whipped back at him stiffly from behind her magazine.

Nik left his seat and sank down in the one beside her. 'We can get through all this…but we have to talk.'

Prudence threw aside the magazine in a temperamental display that she could not suppress. Her emotions all felt as though they were perched on a knife edge. Nik starred at the heart of a welter of conflicting responses. She wanted him to be close, and yet, on another level, she could not resist the urge to push him away and snipe at him. With an unsteady hand she smoothed down the skirt of the elegant black suit she wore. 'Not now, please…'

'I lost a child, too…' Nik breathed in a raw undertone. 'Don't shut me out, *thespinis mou*.'

As she sprang up to take refuge in the sleeping compartment, Nik caught her hand in his. 'What?' she gasped, eyes over-bright and stinging and avoiding the golden challenge of his.

'We can share more than a bed,' Nik told her with disconcerting candour.

Her face flaming, she pulled her fingers free and fled. He had held her through the nights since she'd lost the baby without touching her, while her shameless body tingled and heated to the hard, muscular embrace of his. Had he known how much she longed for him? Here she was, barely speaking to him, and yet that craving for him refused to cease! Her hands curled into tight fists. He was right. There was a barrier between them but it was a much more basic barrier than he appreciated.

Of course, she was not still blaming him for his candour on the score of parenthood a few days before she lost the baby, she thought unhappily. She was not so stupid or short-sighted that she would hold spite on such a score. No, in the aftermath of her miscarriage, she had come to appreciate that she was hurting so badly because she had set herself up for that hurt. Unrequited love was a recipe for disappointment. Worst of all, she was obsessively in love with Nik and she always had been. But when they were just friends she'd had enough distance to keep her pride and her common sense and independence. In short she had learned to get by without Nik very nicely. After their marriage blessing, however, everything had changed and, with it, her aspirations.

Even so, it wasn't fair to blame him for not loving her. He had never offered love. He still did romance as if he had been born to it and had the right move and word for every occasion. Three weeks of being treated like a goddess in their Tuscan hideaway had left her floating on air, so the return to solid earth again had been understandably tough. Nik was never going to love her and she had to learn to live with that. They could be really close in other ways, she reasoned fiercely. Pride was making her push him away but she did not want to destroy their marriage; she did not want to lose him. Half a loaf still felt better than no bread at all.

'I had a nap…I'm feeling better,' she hastened to assure Nik with a determined smile as they moved through Athens Airport. 'I'm sorry I've been so out of sorts.'

'The experience you've had, you've been a saint,' Nik pronounced, his charismatic smile making her heart bounce like a tennis ball.

She was very much surprised when an older man with a familiar face stepped forward to greet her with solemn formality and ask if he might take her luggage for her. She recognised him as her grandfather's chauffeur.

'My goodness…I'm afraid I wasn't expecting to be met off my flight.'

Nik explained that they had made their own arrangements to travel to the funeral.

'Do you think the driver did that off his own bat?' Prudence asked when they reached their own limo. 'Grandfather's staff were very nice to me when I stayed with him.'

In Nik's experience staff, no matter how kind or well-intentioned, rarely took such initiatives. Were Theo's legal executors keen to cast a polite public veil of concealment over the late tycoon's brutal treatment of his grandchild? A limo ride to the funeral would have been cheap at the price. His handsome mouth took on a sardonic curl. He considered that the more likely explanation.

From the airport they went to Nik's family home, where they had been invited to lunch with his parents. Prudence had received several sympathetic phone calls from her mother-in-law and Nik's sisters and had been warmed by their friendly acceptance. Nik's father also accompanied them to the church.

During the church service, Prudence became conscious that quite a few people seemed to be craning their heads to look in her direction. At the cemetery, the surge of her regret for the fact that she'd never got to know the older man sent tears rolling down her face. Theo Demakis had been her last living relative and to the last he had been a stubborn, bitter, unforgiving man who had rejected her every attempt to treat him like a family member. Of course, that had been his choice, she reminded herself ruefully. While Nik was engaged in dialogue with his father, Gregoly Lelas approached her to check that she was coming back to the Demakis villa outside Athens.

Prudence was surprised by the question. 'I wasn't planning to,' she told her grandfather's lawyer.

'But you are the only possible hostess. Everyone here will be your guests,' the older man pointed out, as if there was nothing extraordinary about her taking a place that had been denied her during his employer's life. 'I would also welcome the opportunity to read the will.'

The concept of acting as hostess at the palatial Demakis villa shook Prudence, but she could not see that she had any choice in the matter if it was expected of her. Her eyes widened a little at that reference to the will. Had her grandfather left her something? A small token? Or possibly some item that might act as an unspoken rebuke for the disappointment she had brought him while he was alive, she thought wryly.

'I can't accompany you,' Nik breathed in a taut undertone of apology when she explained. 'I was content to offer my respects at the funeral but it would be inappropriate for me to enter the Demakis home.'

'But you're my husband,' Prudence protested in dismay at the prospect of being left to cope alone with so many strangers.

'I hate to disappoint you...however, circumstances are such at this moment that I could not be present, *thespinis mou*.' Nik grasped her hand, his thumb massaging her wrist in a soothing gesture. 'The limo will drop me off at my office and return to wait for you until you are ready to leave. I'll be at my apartment by six.'

Feeling that she had been selfish and thoughtless to expect more concessions from Nik when he and her grandfather had parted in such acrimony, Prudence managed an understanding smile. In any event, the number of guests arriving at the Demakis villa kept her too busy to notice Nik's absence. It was still a shock, however, to lift her head and see Cassia Morikis gliding towards her like visiting royalty. With her shining fall of platinum-blonde hair tumbling round her slender shoulders and wearing an impossibly elegant little black dress and hat, Cassia looked like an exquisite doll put on earth purely to depress other women.

The blonde woman settled sparkling brown eyes on Prudence. 'A lot of people were very impressed that Nik attended the funeral. He has so much class. You'll never match him. You didn't notice me at the service, did you? You were too busy looking devout.'

'The church was crowded.' Prudence fought to maintain her composed front, even while her tummy lurched as if she was in a tiny boat spinning in a whirlpool. She had always found the blonde intimidating and that teenaged fear of humiliation was with her still. 'I wasn't aware that you were acquainted with my grandfather.'

'Weren't you? My father has been a powerful man in Demakis International for several years.' Cassia, who was on the best of form, gave her a sickeningly smug smile. 'Of course, the will may not have been read but we all know that Theo has left the lot to his first wife's cousins in Germany. They don't need the money and they'll leave the business in the capable hands of the current management. Nice for us, but not so nice for you.'

As Prudence had never been under the impression that she would inherit her grandfather's wealth, Cassia's spite had no effect on her. 'If you like to think so.'

'Oh, I do.' Cassia laughed softly. 'I'm amazed that you can act as though you belong in this house. Whose sad idea was that? After all, you weren't welcome here when Theo was alive.'

'I'm amazed that you still hate me so much,' Prudence confessed truthfully. 'The past eight years must have been very empty for you if you're still so bitter about Nik and I getting married—'

'And what sort of a marriage is it?' Cassia cut in furiously, twin spots of high colour burning over her delicate cheekbones. 'Just a big fat fake! I did him a good turn when I ensured that he flaked out on your wedding night. Beautiful Nik, forced to marry someone ordinary and boring like you—'

Prudence's soft blue gaze had turned to steel. 'You...ensured?'

'Who else?' Cassia could not conceal her triumph. 'I slipped the pill into his drink when he wasn't looking.'

Prudence trembled with rage. She remembered that Nik had said how much he cherished the fact that she never forgot she was a lady. She remembered that it was a solemn and sad occasion. She also strove to recall that violence was not an answer to a difficult situation. She breathed in so deep as she restrained herself that she almost went into orbit.

'Mrs Angelis…' Gregoly Lelas interposed at a most welcome moment. 'Would you like to come into the library now?'

Prudence was bemused to find that she was alone in the room with three lawyers. 'Where is everyone else?'

'There are no other beneficiaries,' she was told and before the significance of that statement could sink in the will was read.

'I don't think I quite understand.'

'You have inherited the entire estate and are now an extremely wealthy woman,' Mr Lelas clarified with assurance.

'But the cousins in Germany…' she said weakly.

'A cover story that amused your grandfather. You have been an heir to the Demakis holdings since the day that your father, Apollo, died.'

Prudence was shattered by that statement. 'But that was more than fifteen years ago…and at one stage my grandfather believed he had a second son.'

'Yes. But even during that period you would still have inherited a substantial share of Mr Demakis's estate. You have Demakis blood in your veins and that meant a great deal to him.'

The shock Prudence had received was so great that she felt numb and unresponsive. 'But my grandfather wasn't even speaking to me…'

'Mr Demakis was a very complex and clever man and not always easy to understand.' The lawyer and his colleagues went on to list the main assets of the estate; ten minutes later they were still talking and Prudence's lower lip felt permanently parted from the upper.

'Obviously we will need to have a series of meetings as there are many formalities to be observed.'

'Obviously,' Prudence echoed, a slightly glazed look in her eyes.

'I don't wish to tax you with more today. Shortly before Mr Demakis died he made a short film that he wished you to view.'

'A film? He knew that he was ill?'

'Yes. He preferred that his fragile state of health towards the end of his life remained a private matter.' The lawyer passed her a DVD in a sealed case, indicated the player and announced that he and his colleagues would wait outside to answer any questions she might have.

With a thudding heart, Prudence broke the seal, extracted the DVD and fed it in. The image of her grandfather flicked up on screen. It was a good five years since she had seen him in the flesh, and age and poor health were etched in his grim pallor.

'How does it feel to be an heiress and hold your husband in the palm of your hand?' Theo Demakis asked with a sardonic smile. 'As this film is being made, you and Nik Angelis are sunning yourself in Italy and carrying on like newly-weds. You can thank me for that development.'

'No…you can't have known!' Prudence gasped in stark disconcertion that the older man could have found out about their Tuscan honeymoon.

'Picking a fight with Nik was not difficult. He's very loyal to you. When I evicted you and your menagerie from that squalid house, Nik raced to your rescue as I knew he would. It brought you together. Adversity brings out the best in Nik. So I put him under financial pressure by poaching contracts from his company. He fought back. He even sold his yacht to fund the purchase of Oakmere Abbey. How chivalrous of him.' The older man shook his grizzled head in wonderment. 'Since then, as you're no doubt aware, Demakis International's campaign to put your husband's company out of business has been steadily gaining ground. I knew Nik wanted to feel free of my influence and I gave him good reason to believe he had succeeded.'

'Oh, my word…' Prudence mumbled sickly, for a hundred and one things were falling into place for her and she was aghast at what she was hearing. On more than one recent occasion, she had marvelled at the endless hours of work Nik put in and the frequent phone calls he made and received. Indeed, she had scolded him for his preoccupation with business and his exhaustion. But he must have been worried sick, for her grandfather was a formidable opponent. How could she not have guessed what was going on? And how could he not have told her?

'And now Nik is yours and you can call all the shots, Prudence. That is how I always planned it,' her grandfather assured her.

'That's not possible!' Prudence gasped in disbelief.

'You're a Demakis. I'm making you a very rich and very powerful woman,' Theo Demakis continued with satisfaction. 'If I'd known how stubborn you are, I might not have used the tactics I did eight years ago. But it offended me to see in a girl the traits that your father, Apollo, lacked. You have his sentimentality but not his weakness. You should acknowledge that I chose you the perfect husband. '

As the recording concluded, Prudence went into shock and stared into space, her brain teeming with frantic half-formed thoughts. Her most overriding need was to see Nik but first she tackled Gregoly Lelas. 'Demakis International is trying to put my husband out of business. What is the position now?'

'I know I may speak for the board when I say that the directors have no desire to continue what has been seen as a personal vendetta,' he responded smoothly. 'But the position is essentially what *you* choose to make it. Theo made his own decisions. He led very much from the front. When the terms of his will are publicised, Demakis International will need a strong guiding hand.'

Nik, she thought numbly. Nik's would be the guiding hand, just as Theo Demakis had always intended. And the whispers of her incredible inheritance had already begun to travel; she saw it in the stunned light in certain eyes that turned towards her, as the crush of people parting allowed her to cross the hall and leave unimpeded. She realised that the news would spoil Cassia's day and that knowledge gave her a wickedly pleasant sensation.

She got into the limousine. *I am rich.* She shook her head a little to clear it but the floating sensation of unreality persisted. This time around, she was going to save Nik, and that had a certain poetic justice.

Nik was chatting on the phone when she found him. His dark eyes flared gold when he saw her standing on the threshold of the large airy reception room. A smile curving his handsome mouth, he stretched out a lean brown hand to welcome her to his side. Willingly she grasped that hand and let him fold her up against his hard muscular frame while he completed his call in husky fluent French that made her toes curl.

'How was it at the house, *pethi mou*?' he asked softly.

'Not so bad…but Cassia was there and less than pleasant.'

'Nothing new in that.'

Prudence eased round to look up at him in surprise at that quip. 'Well, guess what? Cassia also admitted that she spiked your drink on our wedding day.'

Nik raised a questioning black brow. 'How did you get her to confess? Thumbscrews and a rack?'

'She couldn't resist the urge to crow about it—'

His wide, sensual mouth hardened. 'What a bitch,' he murmured with contempt. 'I suspected it but I didn't think I'd ever know for sure.'

'To be frank, I want to discuss something rather more important than Cassia…' Prudence ran possessive fingers down over the lapel of his beautifully cut jacket. 'I understand that my grandfather spent the last few weeks of his life trying to put you out of business.'

Nik stiffened and set her back a step to scan her oval face. 'How did you find out?'

'You'd never believe it if I told you,' Prudence sighed, thinking of the recording that had allowed Theo Demakis to speak from beyond the grave. 'Obviously it's true. But I can't understand why you didn't tell me yourself—'

Nik frowned. 'Of course you can understand. You're my wife. He was your grandfather. The situation would have upset you.'

'Yes but—'

'I couldn't allow that to happen. It was my duty to protect you.'

'By keeping me in the dark for weeks on end? It actually makes me feel quite foolish. I'm not a little kid, Nik. I also feel that I'm an equal in this marriage, and that if you think it's your job to protect me I think it's my job to be supportive when times are tough.'

'That's sweet, *thespinis mou*.' Nik dropped a kiss down on the crown of her head as though she was the child she had denied she was. He was so close she could smell the evocative scent of his skin and it sent a trail of sensual messages winging through her sensitised body. 'But if I'd told you what was happening, it would have wrecked our honeymoon. Then you had the shock of the miscarriage to deal with. You would have fretted yourself to death. I couldn't allow that.'

'But I had a right to know—'

'I won't apologise.' He released the clip that restrained the chestnut fall of her hair at the back of her neck and encouraged the thick, silky strands at the front to curve round her flushed cheekbones. 'If I had the same choice again, I would behave in the exact same way—'

'No, you wouldn't—'

'We have a real marriage now. It was important that we spent time together in Italy and that nothing spoiled those weeks. Also, that you recovered fully from losing our baby—'

'But you shut me out of what was really happening in your life—'

Brown fingers turned up her chin, brilliant dark golden eyes colliding with hers. 'You shut me out when you lost our child…'

'I did…didn't I?' Prudence conceded, her throat thickening with tears.

'You were hurting and I wanted to help and you wouldn't let me. I'd never thought of a child as something missing from my life,' Nik admitted tautly. 'But when I thought of you having my baby inside you, it blew me away. Right up until the last minute I prayed there would be a miracle and you wouldn't lose our child.'

'Oh…' Prudence was initially silenced by that admission, for his sincerity was indisputable. As she looked up at him, her blue eyes shone over-bright. 'You did? So did I,' she confided gruffly.

'Whenever you're strong enough and you feel that the time is right, I want to try again, *thespinis mou.*'

She swallowed hard, happiness slanting through her like a

burst of sunlight on a dull, overcast day. And what better day to celebrate the possibility of new life? she asked herself feverishly. 'Grandfather would have been really pleased—'

'I'm sure you'll understand that I mean no disrespect when I say that Theo's tyrannical wants and wishes were and are a matter of supreme indifference to me.'

'Yes, you're entitled to feel that way.'

'How do you turn me on so hard and fast?' Nik gritted, hauling her close with impatient hands and lowering his proud dark head to possess her luscious pink mouth with a driving sexual passion that made her knees go weak.

'There's just one thing I should mention,' Prudence broke free to mumble through reddened lips.

'Can't it wait?' His breath fanning her cheek, he let his teeth graze her full lower lip. When he dipped his tongue into the moist interior of her mouth in a powerfully erotic invitation she gripped both his arms to keep herself upright.

'I think you'll want to hear that you don't have to worry about Demakis International destroying your company any more,' she whispered with a sunny smile. 'Am I right?'

'I hate to disappoint you, *pethi mou*,' Nik husked, 'but I'd pretty much worked that out for myself. The same day that Theo passed away the dirty-tricks campaign ground to a sudden halt. Such a battle made no economic sense.'

Feeling a little cut off but grateful for the news all the same, because she still could not get her head around the reality that she now owned Demakis International, Prudence muttered, 'That's great. I'm relieved.'

Nik scooped her up into his arms and carried her down the corridor into an imposing masculine bedroom furnished in contemporary style.

'You know, I got quite a surprise when the will was read,' she began. 'Cassia had mentioned these German cousins—'

'Everybody's heard of them. Rich as Croesus, and as old as the hills.' Nik stole a long, lingering, passionate kiss and slowly lowered her down on the bed. 'Theo would have been wiser leaving his ill-gotten gains to some charitable endeavour.'

Prudence sat up on her knees. 'Or…to me?' she suggested uncertainly.

Nik laughed with rich appreciation. 'You were never in the running. I don't think I'd like a wife rich enough to buy and sell me ten times over.'

'Are you absolutely sure of that?'

Nik stared down at her, lush black lashes of extraordinary length merely accentuating the depth and clarity of his clear gaze. 'Why are we having this conversation? Were you disappointed at being left out of his will?'

'No… because I wasn't…left out, I mean.'

Nik frowned. 'What did Theo leave you? Some family memento? I'm surprised he left you anything.'

'He left me everything.'

Nik froze. '*Theos mou*…you cannot be serious.'

'Everything: the houses, the cars, the jewellery, the businesses, the jets, the yacht.'

Nik studied her in unconcealed shock and then he spread his powerful arms in a movement of acceptance, dark colour lying in a line along his superb cheekbones. 'If you say it is so it must be so, but I can hardly credit it—'

'Wait until you see the recording he made.' Her announcement made, Prudence scrambled off the bed and pelted back to the lounge to remove the disc from her handbag.

Having followed her, Nik extended a hand and took it from her. 'Theo filmed himself—'

Sudden misgivings assailed Prudence as she recalled some of the inflammatory things that her grandfather had said. 'I don't think you should watch it—'

'Why not?' Nik enquired almost lazily.

The tension in the air made her heartbeat speed up. She was appalled at how thoughtless she had been in bringing the recording to his notice. 'You never got on with him—'

'Neither did you…or the rest of the human race for that matter. What did he say about me?'

Prudence was rigid. 'Why should you assume that he said anything?'

'If Theo took the trouble to make a film, it was to gloat about how clever he was.'

'Look, it's mine and I would like it back…' Awkwardly she stuck out her hand.

'No…I insist on watching it.' Nik shot her a wrathful glance of challenge.

And he did.

Prudence hovered in an agony of horror and shame. From the first cringe-making words, when Theo gloried in having made her an heiress who held her husband in the palm of her hand, she saw Nik turn white below his vibrant bronzed skin tone and she felt sick.

'Nik…don't let him get to you—'

Nik slashed a silencing hand through the air. She could feel the rage vibrating through him while her grandfather delineated his every move.

'He's right…I was a prize fool,' Nik growled.

'No, he's wrong…you're a very different man from him and I wouldn't want you any other way. Please don't watch any more of this.'

But he paid her no heed. His classic profile set granite-hard, he watched the film from start to finish and then replayed it to ensure that her interruptions had not caused him to miss a single poisonous word. Finally he swung back to her, his golden eyes glittering as dangerously as the heart of a furnace, aggressive energy written in every line of his lean, beautifully balanced body. 'If you keep the money, I walk…'

Prudence just stared at him, certain she had misheard, misunderstood, mis-something, anything that could convince her that he was not serious. 'You don't mean that.'

'You're not going to miss what you've never had or what you never expected to possess, *thespinis mou*.'

'That's not the point. You're just mad because Theo said all that stuff and it was offensive.'

'Once you suggested that I might regard you as a financial asset. I will not be known as the husband of the Demakis heiress.'

'Well, you are!'

'Not if I choose not to be. Don't tell me greed has got to you already,' Nik breathed with ringing scorn.

'I don't have to justify myself to you. I'm a Demakis.'

Nik shot her a derisive appraisal.

'I meant that Theo was my grandfather and that's why he wanted me to inherit his estate. He acknowledged me. He may have waited until he died but he finally allowed me to feel like a member of his family and I'm not going to reject everything he spent his whole life working for,' Prudence protested in a sudden feverish bout of self-defence.

'Then you have a problem. I will be no woman's kept man.'

'Maybe you should wait until you get the offer to be one!' Prudence shot at him, frantically blinking back tears. 'I owned virtually nothing but the clothes I stood up in when we got married and I had to live with it—'

'You lived with it so well, you fled to another country!'

'How can you throw that at me again?'

'Once a Greek husband, always a Greek husband, *glikia mou*.'

'I'm going to be rich…and I'm going to enjoy every minute of it!' Prudence told him defiantly.

'But not with me…'

The words hung there in cold, confrontational challenge and she blenched. She was so furious with him that she felt light-headed with sheer rage.

'So you don't want to be married to the Demakis heiress? OK, if that's how you feel, I'll go back where you seem to think I belong!' Pausing only to retrieve the DVD and tuck it back in her bag, Prudence walked out to the hall. Her overnight bag was sitting there. She lifted it. She gave him lots and lots of time to say something to stop her. Something like, Where are you going? or, Come back here, or even, Let's talk about this tomorrow. The terrible silence roared in her ears like the quiet before a hurricane and perspiration dampened her short upper lip. The sound of the apartment door banging shut behind her shook her.

She took a cab back to the Demakis villa and swanned in as though she had always lived there. The staff still on duty were assembled and formally introduced to her. The cook promised her a special supper calculated to tempt the most delicate appetite and the housekeeper showed her into a magnificent bedroom suite with a balcony that overlooked the garden. She went for a shower and put on a light wrap.

Why was she feeling so devastated? She was furious with Nik and she had every right to be! Supper arrived on a tray. Stress always made her want to eat but when she looked at that food and thought of never, ever being held in Nik's arms again she felt sick with fear. She wanted Nik. She craved Nik. This was crazy. He had fought to keep her as his wife. He had forced her to stay as his wife and to live with him. He took marriage very seriously. He could not just suddenly decide to let her go solely because she had inherited a lot of money…*could he*?

Could he really be so diabolically unreasonable? He was stuffed full of macho reactions and ferocious pride. With reluctance she recalled his raw admission that, eight years earlier, he had been taunted about what a good financial catch she would be. What a prophetic warning that had been! Well, she already knew that Nik wasn't after her money, she thought wretchedly. No decent male would want to be labelled a fortune hunter. She could understand that but she could not understand that he could be prepared to abandon her and their future together on the strength of a principle.

Dogs were barking frantically in the grounds that surrounded the villa. The sound of the commotion prompted her to walk out onto the balcony that overlooked the gardens. A security man came to apologise for the noise. He explained that a man had been seen climbing in over the wall, and that there had been a chase, but the intruder had got away.

Prudence got into bed and lay there getting madder and madder. But underneath the anger was a vast, spreading well of terrified insecurity and fear. She loved Nikolos Angelis to bits. She adored him. She had been so, so happy with him, but she had let a crack appear and a distance develop when she'd turned away from him after her miscarriage. That gulf had only lasted for a few weeks but it had strained their relationship and left a vulnerable spot. *I lost a child, too,* he had said. Maybe he was still angry about the way she had reacted. She should not have left the apartment in a temper; she should have stayed.

Exhaustion sent her to sleep in bursts. Around dawn an idea that at first seemed crazy came to her. She ran it round and round inside her head until it no longer seemed quite so off the wall. She could do to him what he had done to her. She could put pressure on him through his company. Why not? What did she have to lose? What was pride if it meant life without Nik?

The delicate, summery blue dress she put on had a neck-line that dipped in a flattering V at back and front. She examined herself from all angles and was extra-careful with her make-up. He would be at his office in Athens. He was there a couple of days a month and she had planned to start accompanying him on the trips. Of late, she had developed an embarrassing tendency to pine when he was out of sight and touch for longer than ten hours. All the barriers had come down and love had got a firm and increasingly desperate hold on her. But when Nik heard what she had to say, he would be surprised and she had not the slightest idea how he would react...

Before Prudence could go out, Cassia Morikis arrived at the gate and asked to see her. On the brink of turning down the request, Prudence changed her mind and received the beautiful blonde in the vast expanse of the formal drawing room. Encouraging her visitor to relax and feel at home was not on her mind.

Looking unusually subdued, Cassia fixed anxious brown eyes on her. 'I'm sure you know why I'm here. I'm afraid I drank too much yesterday and I was very rude to you.'

Prudence knew very well that the other woman must have panicked once she realised that Prudence was now her father's employer. 'Yes, you were.'

'I hope you'll accept my apologies,' Cassia murmured plaintively. 'I'm sure that Nik would want you to forgive me.'

'Nik couldn't care less. I told him who spiked his drink,' Prudence countered drily, watching dismay and embarrassment flare in the blonde's gaze. 'But I assure you that I won't hold your behaviour against your father.'

Minutes after Cassia's hasty departure, Prudence left the villa, propelled by her determination...

CHAPTER TEN

WHEN PRUDENCE ENTERED Nik's cool contemporary office, her heart rate speeded up as if she was running a sprint.

As Nik's stunning dark golden eyes collided with hers, an electric jolt of attraction flamed through her. His lean, darkly handsome face broke into a smile as he strode towards her. 'You are very welcome, *thespinis mou*.'

Wrong-footed by that unexpected salutation, Prudence went pink and worried that he assumed her visit meant surrender to his terms.

'Would you like a tour of the building?' Nik enquired smoothly, for it was her very first visit to his offices in Greece.

Prudence tensed. 'Perhaps later. I came here because I have something important to tell—'

His slumberous gaze wandered from the moist fullness of her lips to the luscious curve of her breasts and back up again in an act of bold appreciation. 'I like the dress—'

'Please let me say what I have to say,' Prudence cut in a touch unsteadily, liquid heat pooling in her pelvis and making her press her thighs together. It shook her that he could awaken desire in her so easily with a certain look or the dark resonance of his husky voice.

With a graceful movement of one hand that signified assent

to her wish to talk, Nik leant back against his glass desk and regarded her with an intimidating level of expectancy.

'I place a very high value on our marriage,' Prudence told him stiffly.

'That's good.'

'So if you don't come back to me—'

Nik shifted long, graceful fingers. 'But I haven't gone anywhere—'

'Don't interrupt me. If you destroy our marriage I will allow Demakis International to destroy your company,' Prudence completed tightly and she was holding herself so rigidly that her knees began wobbling.

Nik studied her in fulminating silence, dark eyes shorn of gold and gleaming, his big, powerful frame motionless and still apparently relaxed.

'You think I won't do it but I will!' she swore shakily. 'We were very happy together and money shouldn't be allowed to come between us.'

'I should have known what I was doing when I blackmailed a Demakis into making our marriage real. You learn fast, *pethi mou*.'

Prudence sucked in a steadying gust of oxygen, her nerves leaping like jumping beans. She had done it. She had threatened him just as he had once threatened her with the loss of all she held dear. But she was appalled at herself, sick inside, ashamed.

Dry-mouthed, she said, 'So what do you say?'

'Bring on the big guns.'

Her cheeks flamed, her tummy flipping. 'That's not a serious response.'

Nik continued to regard her levelly. 'It is. Coercion doesn't work with me. Do you think Theo didn't try it?'

Her throat felt very tight. 'So you're saying…no?'

'I'm saying no.'

She could feel the colour draining from her face. Suddenly the solid ground beneath her feet was vanishing, for she had backed herself into a corner from where there was nowhere else to go. But she lifted her head high, tilted her chin and shrugged as if his response was a matter of near indifference to her. Turning on her heel, she began to walk away.

'But if you were to ask me to be with you of my own free will,' Nik murmured almost roughly, 'I think we could work something out very easily.'

Eyes glinting with tears, Prudence froze in her tracks.

'I missed you last night,' he added gruffly.

She gulped and drew in a long, slow, shaky breath before she spun back to face him again. 'You…did?'

'I've got incredibly accustomed to being married.'

'Have you?' There was a sob trapped in her throat. She had plunged from the heights down into the depths, and was now somewhere back in the middle, terrified of making assumptions.

'I acted like a jerk yesterday. I let Theo get to me.'

Prudence was starting to breathe again. 'I don't blame you for being mad—'

'There was a special delivery waiting for me when I arrived in the office this morning. There were two copies of that film—'

'My goodness, Grandfather sent one to you as well?'

'Watching it again, I retrieved my sense of humour, *thespinis mou*. I took so much care to keep our reconciliation private and it was crazy to do that. It should not have mattered to me that doing what I wanted meant that I was also doing what Theo Demakis wanted me to do,' Nik imparted wryly.

'That was always an obstacle between us.'

'*Ne*…yes, when I was younger. But not any more. I like to

think I'm grown up now.' There was a rueful twist to his wide, sensual mouth. 'Although I felt distinctly boyish last night when my romantic attempt to make a surprise visit on my wife was rudely concluded by a bunch of slavering, attacking dogs and over-zealous security guards.'

Her soft blue eyes widened in astonishment as she recalled the late-night disturbance at the Demakis villa which had sent the dogs crazy, and she gasped, 'That was *you* last night?'

'That was me,' Nik confirmed.

She unfroze and launched herself forward to close her hands over his. 'Why didn't you say who you were?'

'It wouldn't have been cool—'

'I *so* wanted you to come,' Prudence framed in a wobbly voice. 'If I'd known that you were out there, so close to me—'

'I had a very important meeting first thing today…then I was planning to drive over and make a conventional entrance—'

'If only I'd known that…I need never have come here—'

'But what a joy it is to me to know that you would fight for me, too, *pethi mou*,' Nik slotted in, drawing her closer with lean, strong hands, his classic bronzed features taut and serious.

'A joy?'

Dark golden eyes looked down into hers with a light that warmed her. 'There is something that I should have said a long time ago, something I have never said to any other woman. I love you…'

Her full pink lips parted. 'You mean it?'

'More than anything. For the space of a moment yesterday I let my pride rule me and I acted like a jerk, but I never stopped loving you…and I don't believe I ever could.'

She was so tense she could barely inhale as she looked up at him, desperately striving to see the proof of his words in his lean, darkly handsome face. And there it was in his beautiful eyes: all the depth of emotion, affection and sincerity that she could ever have dreamt of seeing there. He found her mouth and the passion that never failed to ignite blazed but this time it was laced with a new deep trust and affection that was no longer concealed.

'Let's get out of here…' Nik said raggedly, linking her hand to his.

The city traffic was horrendous but it didn't bother them too much, because they were too busy kissing to notice.

'When did you fall for me?' she finally asked, when she had to push him away to get some breath back into her lungs and held him at bay with a staying hand.

'I don't know…I honestly don't,' Nik groaned, contenting his need for constant physical contact by lifting her hand to his mouth and lazily sucking on one finger at a time. 'We were friends first. But there was always the barrier of not knowing what had gone wrong between us on our wedding night and that kept it strictly platonic—'

'I so wish I'd talked to you now…but I was hurt and embarrassed and I honestly did think you'd got drunk because you were so unhappy at having to marry me—'

'No…I was not at all unhappy. In fact, at the altar I was struggling to suppress a lust-fuelled fantasy about exactly how I would unveil my virginal bride's lush body,' Nik confessed, making her soft blue eyes widen in shock, and then laughing at her expression. 'Sometimes you are so innocent…'

But, oddly enough, that frank admission did more than anything else to wipe out the old pain and insecurity that had long dogged her memories of that day. Well, she did remember the manner in which Nik's smouldering dark gaze had travelled over her low-cut gown and, although hot colour warmed her complexion, she was pleased that even in those days she had roused his desire.

'And yet so sexy,' Nik growled, manhandling her with intent in the lift on the way up to his apartment. 'I'm always desperate for you…'

Slight colour burnished his hard, slanted cheekbones as another passenger joined them and more circumspect behaviour was forced on them. Nik thrust the door of his apartment open, slammed it shut again and pinned her up against it to claim a hungry, driving kiss.

'We need somewhere with more privacy,' he contended on the way to the bedroom.

'Not my grandfather's villa…it wasn't a happy place for me, so I think we should get rid of it and look for somewhere new where we can live when we're over here…'

Between talking and kissing they made it down onto the bed. Discarding clothes in a frantic rush, they made explosive love, renewing their strong physical hold on each other with joyous satisfaction and relief.

Afterwards Nik cupped her face. 'I love you,' he said fiercely. 'I love you so much. When I thought I might have lost you last night I felt sick…I couldn't sleep. You have come to mean so much to me.'

'I love you, too…I can't believe I've never said that to you before—'

'You've never said it. Our marriage had too poor a start.'

'Don't look back,' Prudence murmured adoringly. 'You weren't ready then for that amount of commitment.'

'But I'm really committed now. When you said you wanted a divorce, it was some wake-up call. I went haywire; I didn't know what was the matter with me, but suddenly I knew that I would do anything sooner than let you go. But you were so determined…and the sperm-bank idea really wiped me out—'

Prudence ran possessive fingertips down over his bronzed,

muscular chest and smiled helplessly. 'I must admit that you've been a lot more fun.'

'You're getting very bold, Mrs Angelis,' Nik censured huskily, bending over her to circle her lips with his in a skilful foray. 'I love bold…'

EPILOGUE

TWO YEARS LATER, Nik called in at the veterinary surgery he had asked to look out for a dog for him. One of Prudence's Labradors had recently passed away and he had decided to look out for a potential replacement for her. Well acquainted as he was with her views, he knew that both puppies and pedigrees had the easiest time finding a home and that any animal he picked should fall outside those two categories.

'I waited until I had a choice of four gathered up for you,' the vet told Nik, leading him out to the kennels. 'It'll be a very lucky dog that gets a home with Mrs Angelis.'

'This is Doodle. He's in good health but old.' The vet grimaced. 'His owner passed away.' A collie-type dog with a venerable greying muzzle wagged a genial tail from behind the wire.

'Milly was in an accident…she has only one eye.' Nik studied the good-natured golden Labrador jumping up to offer him a welcome and smiled before moving on.

'Peanut was found tied to a skip.' A small, shrinking terrier with frightened eyes was trying to efface himself from notice at the back of the kennel.

'And lastly we have Sausage, who lacks the wow factor…' Nik met the large, doleful brown eyes of a shaggy dog with a big body grafted onto incongruously short, stumpy legs. 'Of course, if there isn't a suitable candidate in this lot, we'll have another couple by next week.'

'And these dogs here?' Nik queried.

The vet winced. 'These are the no-hopers. The council will pick them up but they're unlikely to find a home for any of them. I hang on to dogs like these for as long as I can.'

Nik tensed and paled as comprehension sank in. He turned back to study the dogs with greater intensity. The rejects could well be facing the offer of a ticket to that great kennel in the sky, so he needed to make the wisest possible choice.

While Nik was making his selection, Prudence was twirling in front of a cheval mirror, admiring the fit and flow of the burgundy silk evening dress she had put on that bared her shoulders and emphasised her curves. It had taken some hard work to shed the extra pounds she had put on during her pregnancy but she was delighted with her sleek and shapely figure.

Tonight, she and Nik were celebrating their second anniversary since the marriage blessing. Diamonds sparkling at her ears and at her throat, she walked down the corridor towards the nursery. Life, she was reflecting, had been much better than good. Having waited a few months before trying for another baby, she had almost immediately fallen pregnant with twins. Although both she and Nik had been a little nervous during the early stages in case she suffered another miscarriage, everything had gone very well and their son and daughter had been born just a couple of weeks early. Nik had turned out to be a devoted father, who loved to spend time with his children.

Nik had eventually taken over Demakis International but only after Cassia's father and his replacement had messed up as CEO. The board of directors had approached Nik and literally begged, and her grandfather's empire was now mercifully sailing along peacefully with Nik at the helm. Nik had restructured the business and hired a stronger executive team, so that he would not be forced to put in the hours of a workaholic.

Although they necessarily spent more time now in Greece and often flew out at weekends and holidays, their daily lives were still firmly based at Oakmere Abbey, which had now been fully renovated to offer all the luxurious comfort Nik enjoyed. Prudence had been shaken and deeply touched when she found out Nik had signed his main asset over to her when he had feared losing his business. The animal sanctuary had thrived and she had had to hire more staff to cope. She had become involved with local charities and fundraising but she had cut down on those activities after the birth of the twins.

Now, when she looked into the cots in the nursery and saw her children, her heart simply jumped with happiness. Leo, who was finally dating Stella, had acted as a godparent at the twins' christening. At ten months old, Andreus was very much a little boy and his father's son with jet-black curls. His sister, Leora, was smaller but very determined and incredibly pretty with creamy skin and enormous toffee-coloured eyes. Sleeping, they looked adorable and peaceful.

'What are you thinking?' Nik asked from the doorway.

Prudence shook her head, chestnut-brown hair rippling round her creamy shoulders, soft pink mouth curving. 'That when you look at the twins asleep, you would never guess what little rips they are when they're awake—'

'You were so proud when they started crawling,' Nik teased, closing a hand over hers as he drew level with her. 'They're quite something, aren't they?'

She hid a smile at the level of pride he could not hide.

'I can even feel a little sorry for Theo now. We have the next generation he always wanted,' Nik commented.

'Your parents make wonderful grandparents,' Prudence replied.

He tugged her to him. 'I have a surprise for you, *thespinis mou.*'

'But you already gave me this…' Prudence held out her hand to display the beautiful sapphire and diamond eternity ring that sparkled and caught the light.

'This surprise of mine seemed a good idea when I came up with it, but it may not have been as good an idea as I hoped.' With that cryptic utterance, Nik escorted her downstairs. 'I set out to get you a new pet dog.'

Her eyes lit up in surprise. 'You did?'

'It seemed so straightforward.' He explained carefully how he had gone about the challenge.

The internal courtyard seemed at first glance to be full of dogs. Nik strode over to the wall and scooped up a small, shivering mongrel and petted it almost absent-mindedly. Looking a touch defensive, he swung back and began to introduce her by name to the four animals gambolling round her. 'They're all ours,' he completed.

Even Prudence, the eternal dog lover, gaped at that news. '*All*…of them?'

Nik grimaced. 'I couldn't face leaving one behind.'

'That is so sweet,' she told him happily and gave him a huge hug. 'You do such wonderful things for me.'

'Such as?'

'You sold your yacht so that I could have my dream house,' she reminded him.

Nik vented an appreciative laugh. 'And then luckily for me my wife inherited a yacht that was twice as big and twice as fast.'

'Do you know how much I love you?' she whispered.

'I never get tired hearing it, *agapi mou*.' He watched her getting muddy paw prints on her dress and found that he was smiling and couldn't stop smiling. 'I love you more every day.'

When he called her 'my love' Prudence could feel her heart swelling with sheer happiness. They walked back into the house and kissed with intense pleasure in each other before they strolled down to the dining room to enjoy their anniversary meal.

HARLEQUIN®
Presents

The world's bestselling romance series...
The series that brings you your favorite authors,
month after month:

Helen Bianchin...Emma Darcy
Lynne Graham...Penny Jordan
Miranda Lee...Sandra Marton
Anne Mather...Carole Mortimer
Susan Napier...Michelle Reid

and many more uniquely talented authors!

Wealthy, powerful, gorgeous men...
Women who have feelings just like your own...
The stories you love, set in exotic, glamorous locations...

HARLEQUIN®
Presents

Seduction and Passion Guaranteed!

They're tall, dark…and ready to marry!

If you love reading about our sensual Italian men, don't delay.
Look out for the next story in this great miniseries!

PUBLIC WIFE,
PRIVATE MISTRESS
by Sarah Morgan

Only Anastacia, Rico Crisanti's estranged wife,
can help his sister. In public she'll be a perfect
wife and in private, a slave to his passion.
But will her role as Rico's wife last?

On sale April 2006.